TOMMY'S TURN

The Sequel to The Trouble Trilogy

BESTSELLING AUTHORS
E.R. Fallon & KJ Fallon

Please note the spelling used in this book
is American English.

TOMMY'S TURN
Copyright © 2022 by E.R. Fallon & KJ Fallon

Print-On-Demand via Amazon

Cover Design and Interior Format

CHAPTER ONE

New York City
The 1990s

TOMMY SAT WITH his grandmother at the bar in their pub before they opened for the day.

"You know who is to blame for this whole thing, don't you?" Tommy suddenly broke the quiet atmosphere.

Camille O'Brien, and her husband, Johnny Garcia, were who Tommy thought had killed his mother Violet. He more than just thought they had been behind it. Tommy *knew* it. He felt it in his gut.

His grandmother Catherine gave Tommy a look that conveyed she, too, had her suspicions.

"It's about time we fucking did something about it," Tommy demanded.

"Tommy, did those drugs you used to take destroy your mind?" his grandmother asked.

Tommy hadn't taken heroin for six months, back when he hit rock bottom. He finally got clean after passing out during his mother's memorial. Every day it was a struggle for him to resist, and his grandmother knew that, and it seemed as if she liked to hold it against him.

"Tommy, we got nobody with us these days, and they've got a whole crew behind them," his grandmother continued.

But revenge churned deep inside of Tommy. He despised feeling helpless. Helpless about his mother's death, and helpless about making those who'd killed her pay for what they'd done. Tommy rose and went behind the bar, refilled his coffee, and then went about starting to get everything set up for the first part of the day.

Catherine checked the time on the clock, and then stood up to unlock the door for the day's customers. Just as she was starting to sit down again, the door opened and Camille O'Brien's mother, Sheila, walked inside the pub.

Catherine and Sheila had a history between them, with Sheila's Irish gangster husband, Colin O'Brien, having been enamored with Catherine in her younger days. Sheila suspected that the two had had an affair, but never confirmed it. Sheila had remarried twice since Colin's murder and went by the name Sheila Marchesi now.

Tommy took one look at Sheila and nearly spat out his coffee. The nerve of that bitch to come there. Before he could come out from behind the bar and yell at her to leave, his grandmother went towards her.

"What the hell are you doing here?" Catherine asked Sheila. The two tall, shapely, older women were almost identical in height, traces of their once-coveted beauty still very evident on their faces.

"Now, before you try to kill me, you can at least hear what I've come to say," Sheila told them calmly, holding out her hand for emphasis.

"You have fucking nothing to say that we would want to hear!" Tommy shouted as he approached them from the bar.

"Easy, tough guy." Sheila smirked, and he wanted to slap her, but he recoiled because he didn't hit women.

"I came all this way to see you two," Sheila said. "Do you really think I'd risk coming here if I didn't have something really important to tell you, something you'll want to hear?"

"We don't want you here coming here to gloat," Tommy said.

"I haven't," Sheila said, and Catherine looked a little more interested.

Sheila eyed the bar where their coffee cups were.

"Mind if I sit?" she asked them.

Tommy hesitated, but Catherine replied, "Go ahead."

Tommy had to admit that it took a lot of guts for Sheila to enter their pub, alone, and, in a way, he had to admire her. Still, he conveyed his dismay to his grandmother with a scowling look.

Sheila went over to the bar without so much as a glance over her shoulder. She sat down and Tommy looked at his grandmother.

"What the hell are you doing?" he muttered. Tommy disliked how his grandmother was letting Sheila take charge.

Catherine shrugged. While what happened to Violet had taken a toll on both of them, it had seemed to soften Catherine, making her let her guard down slightly. But it had done the opposite to Tommy, hardening him into someone unrecognizable from who he was before.

"I want to hear what she has to say," Catherine whispered to him.

"Make yourself comfortable," Catherine told Sheila. "But I ain't going to offer you a cup of coffee."

Sheila laughed slightly. "Mind if I smoke?" she asked after a moment.

"You still smoke after all these years?"

"Don't you?"

"No, I quit in prison. I don't drink much anymore either."

"Doesn't sound like much fun," Sheila joked.

"What do you want?" Tommy demanded to Sheila, tired of their bantering. The last he'd heard, Sheila and his grandmother hated each other, so why the pleasantries?

"I'm sorry about your mother," Sheila told him, with genuine sympathy in her eyes.

Tommy didn't answer. He kept his wrath hidden deep within himself as he glared at the woman.

Sheila lit her cigarette and elegantly exhaled curls of smoke in the air from her nostrils. "I've been doing a lot of thinking over the past year, and I know Camille has, too."

Camille. Hearing the name shook Tommy's core.

"We're all very sorry about Violet," Sheila said after a pause.

"You don't get to say her fucking name to me!" Tommy shouted.

"Calm down, Tommy," his grandmother intervened.

"You want me to calm down? You invite this woman in here, as if she's our fucking friend, when you've always hated her, and you expect me to just stand here and do nothing?"

Catherine looked embarrassed and Sheila smiled at her.

"It's all right, Cathy," she said. "I always knew you didn't like me." She stared at Tommy. "You shouldn't speak to your grandmother that way."

"He usually doesn't," Catherine replied, and that was true: Tommy had feared the wrath of his mother and grandmother like he feared nothing else.

"Never mind how I talk. Say what you came here to say," Tommy said, wanting Sheila out of there quickly.

Sheila stopped smoking and looked at them, standing and watching as she crushed what was left of her cigarette in the ashtray. "My Camille and her Johnny, they had nothing to do with what happened to your Violet."

Tommy wasn't so sure about that.

He didn't know whether to laugh or scream. "They had nothing to do with what happened? That's a fucking lie," he said instead. "She's fucking lying," he told his grandmother.

"No, I'm being honest with you," Sheila said

calmly. She eyed Catherine. "I wouldn't blame Camille for killing *you* though, after what you tried to do to her in prison."

"What's she talking about?" Tommy asked his grandmother.

"She didn't tell you?" Sheila said. "Your gran tried to shank my daughter when they were at the same prison."

Tommy wouldn't put that past his grandmother, so he said nothing.

Catherine shrugged. "You know how it is, Sheila."

"But Camille won't be doing none of that to you, so there's no need to worry," Sheila said to them. "You can trust us." Sheila, astute business-woman that she was, wanted a truce. "Let's see if we can work things out," she said.

"You expect us to trust you and your fam-ily, after everything you've done to us over the years?" Tommy made a fist and slammed it down on the bar, and Sheila jumped a little.

Tommy stilled when he saw he was frightening her.

Catherine stepped between them. "Why come here now, after all this time? My grandson's right," she told Sheila. "We can't trust you. There's too much history. Leave our pub. Now."

Tommy's tense shoulders relaxed from the sat-isfaction of seeing his grandmother order Sheila away.

Sheila didn't speak as she opened her purse to retrieve another cigarette and her lighter, then rose as she put the cigarette to her lips, lit it, and took a deep breath.

"I'm gonna find out who was really behind this," she told them on her way out.

"What do you think she really wants?" Tommy asked his grandmother when Sheila had left.

"With that family, you never know."

The history between the two families was long and raw, and dated back to the era of Tommy's late great grandfather, Sean McCarthy, who had also been a gangster. Sean had had Sheila's first husband Colin, Camille's father, murdered many years ago. Years after that murder, Camille and Johnny, along with Sheila, had stolen control of the neighborhood rackets that Violet ran with Catherine. Then Violet started dealing heroin, and Tommy got caught up in it, which ultimately caused him to lose his job as a police officer.

"She can't be telling us the truth," Tommy said to his grandmother, but on the inside doubt had started to creep in. He had once wanted Camille and Johnny, and their whole crew, dead. But now he wondered, what if Sheila was right? Then what? Who had done this to his mother? He had to know the truth.

"Let the bitch try to convince us," Catherine replied. "At the very least, it should be interesting," she said, as though she enjoyed making her former competitor suffer. "You know how much I hate that bitch."

"You sure weren't acting like you hated her a moment ago," Tommy said.

Catherine gave him a look that could have killed him. "Just because I didn't take out a gun and maim her when she was in front of me, doesn't mean I like her. It's better to let people think everything's fine between you, even when it isn't. That way, they won't see you coming."

Tommy smiled internally at his grandmother's logic. She certainly was a tough woman. And that was what he loved best about her.

CHAPTER TWO

Dana Fitzpatrick missed being a detective. Sometimes. After all, her father had been a police officer, and it was in her blood. Now, working as a private investigator, Dana had resigned from the police force after betraying Tommy by revealing his crime family's identity to their boss. She had stayed at work for a while, until her heartbreak became too much for her to handle. There were too many memories of Tommy at the police station, and while she could have requested a transfer, there were just too many memories of Tommy that went along with the job in general. So, she had quietly left.

Working as a private investigator allowed her to use her police skills, but at the same time, it had given her a new start.

And what had happened to Tommy? She had heard through her old friends in the police that his mother's death had devastated him and that he had taken over what was left of the family's gangland empire. Dana had wanted to reach out to him as soon as she heard the news about Violet, but she'd been afraid to. The last time she'd seen him, Tommy had made no secret about despising her. What would she have done if he'd rejected her sympathy?

Dana still thought about him often. She had been in love with him, and she wondered if he still thought about her as well. And if he did still think about her, what was he thinking? Something good, she hoped. But it probably wasn't. When he looked at her the last time she'd seen him, the anger in his eyes was so forceful that she couldn't forget it. But how did he feel now that a year had gone by? Had he forgiven her? Even somewhat?

The heroin case she'd been working on last year had never been resolved after the disappearance of Violet McCarthy's boyfriend, Sam Paul, and the subsequent shooting of Violet. Dana wondered whether Tommy had continued running his mother's drug business, but she never looked into it.

Today, she sat in the small office she shared with her assistant, staring out the window that overlooked the city skyline, grimy and gray, despite the shining sun. Her assistant, Brian, was an acting student in the evenings and went to the occasional audition if the part seemed promising.

"Anyone ring us?" Dana heard Brian say as he entered the room and closed the door.

She turned around, looked at him, thin and classically handsome, and shook her head. Business had been slow lately. Very slow.

Brian sighed. "Do you think we're going to go out of business?"

"I hope not," Dana replied. "Things have been slow before."

"Not this slow," Brian remarked, half to himself.

Dana forced a smile. "Let's see what happens. I know you need to pay for your acting classes."

Brian laughed. "I'd miss you, too, you know." He grinned.

There was the sound of two people, a man and a woman, talking in the hallway outside the office. Suddenly, someone knocked on the door.

Business? Or was somebody lost?

"Yeah, come in," Dana shouted, hoping for the former.

Brian opened the door for them then moved out of the way. In the doorway stood a tall man with dark good looks, and a raven-haired woman, attractive in an edgy way, and walking with a silver-handled cane that didn't do anything to temper her toughness. They looked like a couple, and they were dressed like they were well-off. Dana jumped up to greet them.

"Dana Fitzpatrick, private investigator," she said, shaking the man's hand first.

"Johnny Garcia," the man replied, "and this is my wife, Camille."

Camille had an odd smile, and it looked more like a frown, but Dana assumed they were looking for help, and they'd come to just the right place.

"Please, have a seat," she told them, gesturing to the two chairs in front of her desk.

Johnny thanked her then assisted his wife with her expensive-looking black and silver cane as she sat down.

"Brian, make us some coffee, will you?" Dana said to him as she sat down at her desk.

"What can I do for you?" she asked Johnny and Camille.

She already knew who they were, of course. Johnny and Camille, the crime king and queen of their former neighborhood. She'd heard they lived in the suburbs now, but still ran their section from afar. Dana knew they were trouble, and that what they wanted could inevitably bring her trouble as well, but she had many bills—and an employee—to pay.

"We have a situation, have had one for the past year, actually, and we're hoping you can help us. You know who we are, don't you? I can tell by your face." Johnny looked her in the eye. "When I heard you were an ex-cop, I knew we should hire you, because you'd already know who we are, and we wouldn't have to waste time telling you about us. Who we are ain't gonna be a problem, is it?"

"Do you mean, because you're criminals?" Dana asked him slyly.

Camille sat there quietly, watching her. Dana had heard of her brutal reputation on the streets and knew that just because she was silent at that moment, it didn't mean she should underestimate her.

There was a history between Camille's and Dana's families, but Camille didn't seem to comprehend that. Dana wondered whether she should remind her, but now didn't seem like the best time or place to do so. Dana's mother, Lucille Byrne, had been very good friends with Camille's gangster father, Colin O'Brien, when they were younger. Until Colin was sent away to prison and Lucille married the policeman who helped ease her away from the drink.

"Mr. Garcia, I'm no longer a police officer. I work with many kinds of people these days," Dana answered him. "As long as I'm not doing anything illegal, there's no problem with me assisting you."

"So, we can trust you?" Camille finally spoke. She seemed amused by the idea that they should trust a cop.

Dana nodded. They knew she'd once been a cop when they came there, so what was the big deal now? "I'll keep anything you ask me, and anything I find out for you, strictly confidential," she told them.

Johnny nodded, seeming satisfied, but Camille didn't look as sure. Dana assumed that it was Johnny's—and not his wife's—idea for them to come to see her.

"Good, now that we got that out of the way," Johnny said, and it was clear to Dana that he had the final say in the matter, regardless of what Camille might have been thinking, "here's the problem: Around a year ago, this woman was shot, she was killed, and her family thinks it was us. Between you and me, I've done a lot of bad things in my life, but I swear on my father's grave that I didn't do this."

That oath meant a lot. Johnny's father had been

the world to him, even though he was taken from him when Johnny Jr. was very young. He still thought about his father often, piecing together stories his mother had told him with accounts of some of his father's former associates and what he had figured out for himself.

Johnny Garcia Sr. was half-Cuban and half-Irish and had joined Cuban-born Tito Bernal's gang, the *Tigres*. Johnny Sr. had been fast friends with Colin O'Brien, Camille's' father. Even so, Colin had slept with Johnny Sr.'s wife, Bernal's daughter, once. Just the one time, but still…

In the end, Colin had been there during an attack ordered by his gang led by Tom McPhelan in which Tito and his men, including Johnny, Sr., had been killed. The rivalry between the gangs had come to a head and so the violence was ordered.

Colin hadn't shot Johnny, even though Tom had wanted him to kill Johnny to show Colin's loyalty to McPhelan.

Strange alliances, strange histories, with even stranger outcomes, including Colin's daughter Camille's marriage to Johnny Jr.

"With your reputation, I'm surprised you even care what the other family thinks," Dana said.

"I don't like having bad blood with anyone if it isn't justified. It can cause a lot of trouble. The family's son, he could cause us trouble."

"What's the family's name?" she asked.

"The McCarthys. This is Violet McCarthy we're talking about, who died last year. I'm sure you've heard of the family, since you used to be a cop."

Dana felt like she'd been drained of the ability to move. Violet McCarthy, Tommy's mother. It occurred to Dana that they didn't know her connection to Tommy.

"I know who she was, yeah," Dana replied, quietly, after a moment, not giving anything away. Under normal circumstances, she would be legally obligated to declare her connection to the McCarthy family, but because business was slow and she was desperate for money, she remained silent about the matter.

"This shit has been hanging over our heads for the past year," Johnny said. "So I'm sure you understand when I say we'd like the matter resolved quickly. I can give you a thousand upfront." He reached into his jacket and took out a thick roll of bills, flicking through the cash and setting it down on Dana's desk. "Consider this a down payment. You find the answer I'm looking for, you find out who really killed Violet McCarthy, I'll triple the amount. At least."

Basking in the idea of that much cash thrown her way, Dana paused for a moment and then reached across and took hold of the money. She set it down on her desk. Dana hadn't wanted to seem too eager, but she could practically feel Brian beaming at her side.

"Thanks, Mr. Garcia. You're looking to hire someone to find out some information? We can help you, no problem."

Seated next to her husband, Camille didn't look as convinced about Dana's skills as her hus-hand did. "You really think you can help us?" she interrupted. "Or are you just trying to take my husband's money?"

It was clear to Dana that she'd have to work a lot harder to win over Camille.

"I'm very good at what I do," Dana told her. "Of course, there are no guarantees," she added, carefully.

Camille sat up straight and looked at her husband, then pointed at Dana and said, "You see, baby, she's gonna just take our cash and run. Why'd you hand her the money already?"

"Camille, what the hell are you talking about, baby?" Johnny said to his wife. "She's a professional. Right?" he said, looking at Dana.

"Yes, I am," Dana replied to both.

"I told you this wasn't a good idea, Johnny, she ain't even sure if she can help us," Camille said to her husband. "You gonna give us back our money?" she asked Dana.

Dana sat back in her chair and hesitated.

Camille didn't seem to want to be there, and, again, Dana could tell it was her husband's idea to seek help. Perhaps Camille thought they could resolve the situation on their own, but from the uncertain look in Camille's eyes, despite her anger, it seemed like they needed Dana's expertise. How could she convince Camille to hire her?

Johnny sat there, with his hands folded in his lap, staring at Dana, waiting for her to answer his wife. Clearly Johnny valued his wife's opinion and wouldn't agree to hire Dana if she was truly dead-set against it.

Dana knew she had to salvage the situation and clinch the deal. "Believe me, Mrs. Garcia, when I tell you that if there's anyone who can help you, I'm that person." Dana spoke with confidence, although she was a little unsure herself. Because if there was one thing Dana knew very well, it was that there were no guarantees in life, and not many in business, either.

Camille sat still, watching Dana in silence. After a few tense moments, she glanced at her husband and nodded, then said to Dana, "You better succeed," eyeing her closely. She paused. "You can keep the money." Camille pointed at the cash in front of Dana on the desk.

Dana lightly brushed her fingers across the bills. Money always felt so good to touch, no matter how dirty it was.

CHAPTER THREE

————◆————

JOHNNY AND CAMILLE'S daughter, Phoebe, had grown up to be a beautiful nineteen-year-old. She'd finished school a few months ago and was living on her own in a small apartment in the city, despite her parents' objections. She worked at a women's clothing shop nearby. Phoebe just wanted some independence from her family and the burden that came with being connected to them. Her parents had tried to shield her from their gangland lifestyle, but Phoebe was smart enough that she'd figured it out on her own. There were no secrets between them anymore. Of course, the girl didn't know all of the things, good or bad, her parents had done. But she knew a lot of them.

Phoebe had been left shaken ever since her kidnapping at the hands of Camille's ex-stepfather, Vito Russo and his daughter, Marie, as an act of revenge against Camille for destroying Vito's reputation. The ordeal had changed Phoebe, leaving her with a hardened exterior, but on the inside, she was all the more fragile because of it.

She thought back yet again to the night she

was abducted, not that she ever *didn't* think about what had happened about a year ago. Maybe it got pushed back away from whatever preoccupied her thinking her during the present, but what Marie had done to her never really left her.

Sometimes, like now, she remembered it like it had happened yesterday. Phoebe had gone with her mother to see a movie, kind of like a girls' night since her father had been busy and had no interest in seeing a film like *Pretty Woman* anyway. She and her mother had enjoyed the movie and were walking back home, talking about some of the scenes in the movie and just how unrealistic they were, when, not far from their street, a car came out of nowhere, slowly at first and then sped up, then stopped. Someone got out, rushed at her and grabbed her, since she had, stupidly, in a panic, ran out into the street. The attacker then pushed her into the car and started to take off.

It was a woman, Phoebe found out as soon as the car sped away with Phoebe screaming and pounding on the car window. When Phoebe turned and started to grab the steering wheel, the last thing she heard was a woman yelling at her to shut up and then she felt a hard *thwack* on her head.

When Phoebe came to, she was in a room she didn't recognize, sitting on a hard chair, her wrists taped behind her and her legs taped together at the ankles. She could hear a man and a woman yelling in another room. Suddenly a woman opened the door and came at her with a very large knife.

"Who the hell are you and what do you think you're doing?" yelled Phoebe. She was scared, sure, but she was also really pissed off.

"Who am I? You'll find out soon enough," the knife-wielding woman said. Then a man came into the room. "Marie, what do you think you're gonna do? Cut her to pieces?"

At that, Phoebe audibly shuddered.

The woman turned from the man and shouted at Phoebe. "Yeah, and what can you or your ma do about it? Nothin'!"

"Marie," the man said, seemingly trying to calm the woman, "you're not thinking this through."

Marie turned back to the man. "Not thinking? That's all I've been doing. Thinking about how this bitch's mother destroyed you. You haven't been the same since Camille and her mother obliterated who you were."

So this was who these people were. Marie. And her father, Vito Russo, who had once been married to Granny Sheila. Phoebe didn't know what exactly had happened, but that marriage had not ended well.

"Camille's not my mother. She's my stepmother and…"

"Shut up. Who said you could talk? I should've put tape around that mouth."

It seemed to go on like that for a long time, then somehow, her father, Camille, and another guy got in and saved her.

And that's how it went on for Phoebe. She replayed what happened and relived everything from that day as if it never ended.

One day, after a particularly difficult time at work, Phoebe walked to Marie's beauty shop, which was a few streets away from where she lived. Phoebe had known about this when she'd moved there. In fact, the location was the main reason Phoebe had chosen to settle there. Camille and Johnny were unaware of their daughter's intentions.

Phoebe still feared Marie and usually avoided spending much time outside, just going from her apartment to her job and back. But in a way, she was also curious about what had become of the woman who'd nearly ended her life. Did Marie have any remorse? Phoebe doubted it, but she had to see for herself. She didn't plan to speak with her. She felt that just by seeing her, she'd be able to tell.

Phoebe stopped walking a few shopfronts away from Marie's place. She hoped to see Marie leaving for the evening. Phoebe hid in an alleyway between two empty buildings on the quiet street, concealed by the night, the moonlight allowing her to see Marie's shop clearly despite the lack of streetlamps. After a couple of minutes, a woman, in her forties, small, dark-haired and pretty, exited the shop, whistling a cheerful tune to herself as she locked the door. Marie. Marie turned and tossed the keys into the air and caught them easily and confidently with one hand.

What had Phoebe expected to see? Marie, despondent, staring at the ground, shuffling back to her house? Remorseful? On the contrary, Marie seemed to be in very good spirits, and walked in such a way that she seemed to be almost skipping. Remorseless didn't even begin to cover it.

Phoebe hadn't seen her in a year, but she seemed to be doing well for herself, with her beauty shop appearing so well-maintained that she must have had a lot of business. And here was Phoebe, trapped, frozen, in the ordeal of last year, unable to properly get on with her life. Working in a women's boring and dull clothing shop that she really had no interest in. What was in store for her future? How could she get unstuck from the past and how it held her back?

Rage flowed through her veins at the sight of Marie's joy. She would make that bitch pay for what she'd done. She despised Marie more than she did Marie's father. After all, it was Marie who carried out the actual kidnapping. Phoebe's parents hadn't gone to the police after they got her back, because that wasn't what people like them did. And although Phoebe understood why they hadn't, she resented them a little for it as well.

She didn't want to talk with Marie and ask her why. She had too much anger for that. Words, no matter how pointed and sharp, wouldn't be enough. Phoebe wanted vengeance.

Marie came towards Phoebe's direction, and Phoebe held her breath as she pressed her body against the wall to hide from her view.

Marie stopped near the alley, to remove a cig-arette from her purse and light it. Phoebe held herself absolutely still as she waited for her to finish. She breathed out in relief when Marie walked away.

A man walked past the alleyway and whispered, "Hey, sexy," at Phoebe under his breath.

She ignored him and turned the other way in disgust, bracing for him to stop and bother her. When he kept walking away from her, Phoebe stood there in the darkness, with her back pressed against the rough, cool brick wall, and tilted her head back and closed her eyes. She sighed. She wanted revenge against Marie, but she didn't know how to go about it. There was one person she thought could help her.

Camille was Phoebe's stepmother but loved the girl as if she was her own, and Phoebe felt this affection whenever they were together.

The next morning, a Saturday, Phoebe went to her parents' house in the suburbs when she knew her father would be out playing golf with his friends. Her dad's tastes had become significantly more upscale since moving to the suburbs. She wanted to speak with her stepmother alone. She took the train there and after she exited, she walked to the house, stopping for a box of colorful sweets elegantly wrapped for Camille on her way there.

Camille answered the door, wearing her bathrobe.

"Sweetheart, you're here so early," she said to Phoebe with a smile and a yawn.

"It isn't *that* early," Phoebe replied with a grin. "Have a late night?"

Camille laughed at the girl's joke. "You got me a present?" she asked, looking at the pink box in

Phoebe's hands. Camille gestured for her to come inside.

"Some chocolates for you and dad," Phoebe said, holding them out to Camille, as she entered the house.

"You're a sweetheart." Camille thanked her, then asked, "Why aren't you working at the dress shop today?"

"I have one Saturday a month off and today is it."

"And you came to see me. Is something troubling you? There must be a reason for your visit."

"I've got to have a reason to see you?" Phoebe replied.

"No, but you haven't been here in a while."

"I know, I'm sorry," Phoebe said. "I've been so busy with my job." Then she sighed. "And other things." Phoebe's voice began to crack, and tears threatened to push through and stream down her flushed face.

"Sweetheart, what's going on?" she asked with concern, putting the candy on the hall table and taking Phoebe in her arms.

Phoebe debated whether to tell Camille the truth. Would she be angry that Phoebe had gone by Marie's shop? Would she think it too dangerous?

Before Phoebe could make a sensible decision, she blurted out, "I saw her! I saw Marie Russo."

"You what?" Camille asked, pulling quickly away from Phoebe and staring at her in shock.

"I saw her, but she didn't see me. I went to her shop in the city and waited for her outside."

"Phoebe, why would you do something like that? Do you know who her father is? Do you know how dangerous he is?" Camille spoke with so much urgency that Phoebe sensed there was something personal and emotional behind her stepmother's words, and that there was more to the truth than Camille had admitted.

"I know, but I couldn't help myself."

"They've given us enough trouble already, we don't need anymore," Camille said.

"You and Dad are powerful, too," Phoebe said, a little childishly. By then, she knew of her parents' harsh reputation on the city streets. But she also knew who Vito Russo was.

"Phoebe, you can't go around saying things like that. Marie's father, Vito Russo, he's in the fucking mafia. You don't want to make him angry. You can't bother his daughter."

"I don't give a shit who he is, I fucking hate him." She began to sob. "You and Dad…"

"Phoebe, I'm just a fucking Irish kid, Vito ain't gonna be afraid of me. He ain't gonna be afraid of your dad either."

"I hate them," Phoebe yelled.

"I do, too, for what they did to you," Camille said, taking Phoebe in her arms again and holding her close. "And I hate that we can't do anything about it 'cause of who they are. How did you find out where she worked?"

"I knew she had a beauty shop." Phoebe spoke between sniffles. "I found out through some friends what it's called."

"Where is it, anyway?"

"Not far from where I live," Phoebe spoke without thinking.

"What?" Camille said. "Phoebe, please tell me that isn't why you wanted to move to the city."

Phoebe couldn't lie to her stepmother without Camille figuring it out, so she didn't speak.

She figured it out anyway. "It is, isn't it?" Camille said. "Your father thought it was a bad idea for you to live all alone in the city, but I saw how much you wanted to go, so I encouraged him to let you. Now I'm starting to think it wasn't such a good idea." She put her hands gently on Phoebe's shoulders and looked at her. "You have to promise me you will stay away from Marie Russo. If you don't, I'm going to have to tell your dad and we're going to make you move back home."

"I'm nineteen, you can't make me—"

"You know your father," Camille cut her short. "You know he can make anyone do anything he wants," she said, sounding like she spoke from experience. "He'll pick you up and drag you home if he has to."

Phoebe knew her father well, and she acknowledged her stepmother's words with a nod, but she didn't look at her.

"Phoebe," Camille said, touching the girl's chin. "Look at me. Promise me."

"I won't go near her again," Phoebe said quietly, but, on the inside, she wasn't sure if it was a promise she could keep.

"Good," Camille said. "You better not," she added, as though she had some doubts about Phoebe's promise.

"Please don't tell Dad," Phoebe said, squeezing her stepmother's hand.

"I don't like keeping secrets from your father," Camille said. She sighed. "But I know how important this is to you. I won't say anything. Doesn't mean he won't find out somehow," she added. "He always does."

Phoebe embraced her stepmother and thanked her.

Chapter Four

———◆———

TOMMY HAD BARELY woken up when there was a knock at his door. Who the hell was it, at this early hour?

He got out of bed and put on his jeans, went to answer the door without wearing a shirt. Was it an upset lover? There had been a lot of women coming in and out of his life ever since his mother had been fatally shot, women whom he mostly used for sex and some light conversation and company. He didn't feel like he was in the right place to start a genuine relationship with any of them.

Tommy undid the two heavy chain locks only partly, and opened the door a little, checking to see who was there. With his family's history, he had to be careful, as they had many enemies.

He didn't know what to think when he saw his former boss, Lieutenant Andrews, standing there. He hadn't seen or heard from him since Tommy was asked to leave the police force, about a year ago. What did he want? What would Tommy say to him? He couldn't not answer the door. It was obvious he was home since he had already

opened the door enough to see who it was. And
for whoever it was to see he was home. There was
only one thing to do.

Tommy put on the most neutral poker face he
could muster and energetically opened the door,
then smiled broadly as if he seeing his ex-boss
from the police station standing there at his
apartment door was the best thing that could've
happened to him that day.

"Lieutenant Andrews. What brings you here?"
Tommy tried to sound as upbeat as possible, but
he was wondering what the hell he could want.
Had he found out something about what Tommy
had been up to in his new, very un-cop—the
antithesis of cop—life?

Andrews hesitated outside the open door and
was clearly waiting for Tommy to ask him to
come in. Or to maybe ask him to not come in, to
get the hell out of there.

"I know it's a little unusual . . . and awkward,"
his ex-boss began, "but I always felt bad about the
way things went."

Tommy didn't know what to say, so he said, "I
don't know what to say."

"I know," said Andrews. "I just stopped by to
see how you're doing. See if you were okay. I'm
retiring in a month and my wife and I are going
to be moving to Florida, so I…" He paused. "I
mean, you probably wouldn't want to come, it'd
be understandable if you didn't…but I'm having
a small retirement party away from the station at
a bar…just a few of us…" Andrews stopped at
"us".

Tommy wasn't part of that "us" anymore. He hadn't been for a long time. Tommy was, likely unbeknownst to Andrews, as far away from "us" as possible. Tommy had gone to the other side.

But to make the interaction less painful Tommy offered, "Congratulations, Lieutenant Andrews. Where and when?"

Andrews seemed relieved that Tommy at least didn't think the idea was so terrible that he laughed in his face or asked him to leave his apartment.

"I can get you the details. The date hasn't been set in stone yet, but it'll likely be in about a couple of weeks. I can tell you more when I know more myself." Andrews was silent for a moment and looked around casually and uneasily as if trying to find the way to say something else.

Tommy wondered, was Andrews going to say something about Dana? Would she be at the party? He had heard that she left the force and was working as some kind of private detective. How did Tommy feel about that? He had thought he loved Dana once, but that had curdled, dried up, and blown away when he found out she had ratted to his boss about his mother and her involvement with an investigation both he and Dana started working on. He never should have told her the truth. He had been using his father's surname for all of his life.

Tommy had told Dana this after they had made love, in a moment of weakness, he reasoned now. He'd trusted her not to tell anyone. He had wanted to be honest because he thought maybe he could still do the job somehow and not be influenced by his family, or he could just recuse himself from the case. But Dana hadn't seen it that way and neither had Lieutenant Andrews.

"I want to tell you that I was very sorry to hear about your mother," Andrews finally said, abruptly interrupting Tommy's thoughts about the past.

Tommy hadn't seen that one coming.

Once again, he couldn't think of any words. Andrews seemed to sense the discomfort in the air and said, "I mean, she was your mother and the way she died…"

"Went with the way she lived? Is that what you're going to say?" Tommy was getting more than a little angry.

Andrews looked stunned. "No, not at all. The way she died was horrible and even if she was a criminal, she was your mother and she didn't deserve to die like that."

Tommy was somewhat mollified by Andrews's response. But he still had a lot of unanswered questions about how his mother had died. Like, who killed her.

"Are you or anyone on the force going to do anything about it? About how she died and who killed her? I'll bet the answer to that is a big fat *no*." Tommy's words hung in the air like the deafening echo of a gunshot.

"Look," said Andrews, "I came here for two reasons. To tell you that I'm honestly sorry about your mother and to try to make some kind of amends for why you had to leave the force. I understand that you didn't choose your mother, none of us do. Our parents are our parents no matter what they did or who they are."

Tommy was silent so Andrews went on. "As to what the police are doing to find who killed her, you need to know that we tried—are still trying because the case is not closed and won't be until we know who did this." Andrews waited for Tommy to respond.

When he didn't, Andrews continued. "We won't rest until we find her killer or killers. You need to remember that."

Tommy was stung by those last words. But he also realized that Andrews was trying to be honest and Tommy believed that maybe he really did care that Tommy's mother had met a gruesome and violent death. "I do remember. It's not something I'd forget."

It seemed like a good time to close out the conversation and the encounter. "Thanks for coming by, Lieutenant Andrews."

"Bill. Please call me Bill."

Tommy didn't think he'd be seeing Andrews again let alone calling him by his first name. But he went along. "You got it."

"I'll be in touch about the retirement thing. I'll give you a call. You take care, now. Try to stay out of trouble."

Tommy knew there was no chance of that happening. Trouble was all he knew. Andrews turned to leave, and Tommy opened the door and was glad to see the back of him.

CHAPTER FIVE

CAMILLE AND JOHNNY Garcia had supplied Dana with a list of their key associates,
and all of them had checked out. Except for one,
named Anton, who worked with the Russians
and who had built a partnership with Camille
and Johnny over the years.

Anton had been one of the last associates she'd
followed, and while she hadn't been able to confirm his loyalty, she hadn't been able to disprove
it either. The others had been easier to figure out.

One day, she pursued Anton to a restaurant
after he drove away from the house he shared
with his beloved elderly mother. Trailing a man
like Anton in her car wasn't simple, as men in his
line of work were likely to be suspicious, so Dana
kept her distance, always a car or two behind him,
never too close.

Anton drove into the parking garage of the
restaurant, and Dana double-parked on the
street nearby in an available space until she was
sure where he was going. A few minutes later,
Anton emerged from the garage and entered the
restaurant. Dana found a space that gave her an

unobstructed view of the restaurant. The establishment had an outdoor dining area, and with the warm, bright weather, many patrons were eating outside. Dana sighed, as she'd hoped to be able to use the listening device she had with her, which picked up conversations from far away, if Anton had sat outdoors.

Dana debated whether she should go into the restaurant. She was dressed discreetly, but would someone recognize her from her detective days?

After a few moments of sitting in the car, trying to decide, the tall, muscular, and bald Anton exited the restaurant with another man, a slightly shorter, fair-haired fellow, and went to the outdoor dining area. The fair-haired man looked familiar, but Dana couldn't recall why.

The two men sat at an empty table, and straightaway a server approached them. They spoke with the woman, and seemed to be ordering drinks, then after a few moments, the server went inside. They didn't pick the menus up from the table and looked as though they were using the restaurant as simply a place to meet.

Dana crawled into her car's backseat and used the listening device to hear their conversation, carefully directing it at them.

"How are you doing?" the fair-haired man asked Anton. He had a subtle accent, and, hearing him speak, he seemed even more familiar to Dana. "Did you fuck anyone lately you'd like to tell me about?" He chuckled.

Anton laughed. "There's a few good bitches in my life right now. I alternate fucking them every other day, and the best thing is, they don't know about each other!"

Dana could see his salacious grin from where she sat and rolled her eyes. She'd become used to such tough talk during her police days.

The fair-haired man then proceeded to brag about his own victories in the bedroom, and Dana tuned out for a while. As the man spoke, Dana came to realize who he was. He was a local drug kingpin nicknamed 'the Swede', who the police had been attempting to catch for a long time. But, as far as she knew, the man didn't work with the Russians. So, why was he meeting with Anton?

Their conversation become more serious, and Dana started to pay attention again.

"I know how you felt about her, how you used to be in love with her, so it's honorable for you to overlook that for me, for the sake of our partnership," the Swede said to Anton.

"I did. I fucking loved her," Anton replied in a somber tone. "At one point in my life, Violet meant everything to me. I was also close to her son."

"Tommy?"

"Yeah, him. But some offers just can't be refused, you know?"

Dana was stunned. Violet. Violet McCarthy, Tommy's mother?

"I appreciate what you said, Anton, what you've sacrificed, to help me, and I can promise you that you will be rewarded because of it," the Swede spoke.

The server returned to the table with glasses of what looked like wine, and the choice surprised Dana, although the Swede was a sophisticated man on the outside, and she imagined Anton wanted to emulate him.

"You and I both know why this had to be done. Why Violet had to go." He chuckled. "And I ain't done yet. I'm going to take over their whole fucking neighborhood, and get rid of Johnny and Camille, too. Why just have one thing, when I can have everything?" He paused. "That Camille's a nice piece of ass, though, maybe I'll fuck her before I kill her."

His words alarmed Dana, but she kept listening.

"I don't know if that's right, man," Anton said, as though the other man's crass words had put him off. "I mean, she's got a limp."

"You're going to get a cut of everything, so why do you care what I do?" the Swede said, and it sounded as though they were on the verge of an argument.

Anton seemed to not know what to reply, or he was too fearful to, so he said nothing.

"Your boss and his wife," the Swede said to Anton, "are old and ill, and they have no children of their own together. There's no one to carry on. What they have will be all yours soon, and then we'll be working together. I'm gonna give you a piece of everything, so you better learn to like me," he said with a dry chuckle.

"We're friends, brother," Anton replied. "I've got no problems with you."

"That's good to hear. Because if we're gonna

work together, we'll need to set any differences aside."

Then the Swede took a drink from his glass and said something Dana couldn't decipher.

"I agree with you," Anton told him, and Dana didn't know what he'd just agreed with or to.

She decided it was time for her to leave and deliver Camille and Johnny the news: she'd found their betrayer.

Dana wanted to be extra cautious, so she drove to a payphone near an isolated street, where she rang the number Johnny Garcia had provided. She was sure it was a burner phone, and she almost expected no one would answer, but after a few rings, a man said, "Hello?"

"Johnny?"

"Who is this?"

"Dana Fitzpatrick."

"You find something?"

"Can you meet with me today at my office?"

"Sure, give me a half hour."

"Sounds good. Bring your wife with you."

"Maybe."

Dana sighed. She rang Brian next.

"I'm about a half hour away," she told him when he answered. "Two clients are coming in an hour. Get the coffee started—thanks, I know that isn't part of your job," she added, because she knew the young man didn't wish to be treated like a secretary.

Brian groaned, but said, "No problem."

Dana went into her car and drove to her office, which, with the traffic, took her more than half of an hour. She had taken photos and made a recording of Anton's conversation with the Swede, which she planned to play for Johnny and Camille, in case they were too stunned by Anton's betrayal to take her word for it.

Dana had noticed Johnny and Camille's car, a sleek, red sports car, when they had come to her office the other day, and when she arrived at her building, she didn't see it parked outside. She thought they would have arrived before her and that she'd be late, but it looked like they weren't there yet. Dana parked and went inside.

She walked upstairs to her office and found that Brian had already made and set out the coffee.

"Who's coming? Anyone special?" Brian asked, with his usual, high energy circulating in the small room.

"The people who came here the other day, the couple," Dana answered, draping her jacket on the back of her chair. "No one else has come here since then."

Brian frowned. "You're right, unfortunately. Business has still been horribly slow. Do you mean that tough-looking pair? What are they, gangsters?" He laughed like it was a joke, but Dana looked at him and nodded.

"Seriously?"

"Yes."

"I thought you said you'd never work for criminals. I mean, you used to be a cop."

"I said I would never do anything illegal, and I'm not."

Brian gave her an uncertain look, but then

began to quietly sort the files on her desk. He seemed willing to accept Johnny and Camille's business if it kept him clothed and fed with a roof over his head.

A few minutes later, there was a knock on the door, and Dana called out, "Come in."

Johnny Garcia, tall and handsome, wearing an expensive-looking dark suit and a gold chain around his neck, entered, followed by Camille, with a trace of a sneer on her lips. The other time she'd been in Dana's office, she'd had that type of expression as well, defiant-like. Camille clearly wasn't a woman to underestimate as simply Johnny's little wife.

Dana greeted the couple. "Please, have a seat," she told them.

Camille sat down after her husband, as though she still was uncertain of Dana's intentions, tapping the floor with her cane.

"You got some information for us?" Johnny asked. "I'm assuming that's why you asked us to come here."

"With what you're paying her, she better have something for us," Camille muttered to her husband, but Dana heard the words.

"As a matter of fact, I do," Dana said, pointedly, to Camille.

Camille didn't even flinch, let alone apologize. She sat there, staring at Dana, waiting to be impressed.

"When you first hired me, I promised you I would find out who killed Violet McCarthy, and I have," Dana said.

"Don't keep us waiting," Johnny said eagerly.

"The answer is closer to you than you might think," Dana replied. She put the recording in a tape player she had on her desk and pressed play.

The voices of Anton and the Swede filled the room.

"That's Anton," Johnny said. "And the other guy? I don't recognize him. Who is he?"

"I know who the bastard is," Camille interjected. "It's that Swedish guy."

"Violet's supplier?"

"Yeah, him," Camille replied.

"They're working together, Anton and this man," Dana told them. "As you can hear from the conversation, the Swede had Violet killed, and he now wants to take everything from you."

"That fucker!" Johnny said, teeming with rage. "Camille and me, we met with him last year, to discuss him working with Violet. He was supplying her, and she was dealing in our neighborhood."

"I don't want to know more," Dana replied. "But I think we both know the reason behind his actions," she added.

"Whether or not you like it, you're part of it now," Camille said.

"I'll pay you more, if you keep an eye on that Swede for us. We'll handle Anton," Johnny told Dana.

Dana had a very good idea of what he meant by 'handle.' Indecisive, she glanced at Brian, who had overheard the conversation. He nodded at her to accept the offer. Dana's instincts told her to decline, but since she was close to being kicked out of her apartment, she accepted Johnny's proposal.

CHAPTER SIX

———————

TOMMY LEANED AGAINST the bar and glanced out the large window that faced the street. It was late morning, before the afternoon crowd came in for a round or two of drinks to go with lunch. But business had been slower lately. As the neighborhood had changed over the years and became a bit more fancy, its facades less rough, the polished newcomers weren't as eager to step inside an un-trendy pub like *McBurney's*, preferring to spend their money at the wine bar that had opened up across the street.

With his mother gone, Tommy wondered if he should sell the pub. He had heard stories about other business owners and families being offered large sums of money to vacate so that their building could be demolished and new buildings put up in their place. But his grandmother would kill him, perhaps literally, if he even mentioned that idea to her, so he quickly pushed that thought aside. Regardless, they had to let go of their cook and cut back on offering hot food, except for some basic appetizers and "bar food" that Catherine or Tommy could quicky prepare, if needed.

His grandmother had stepped out to buy a few things from the shops, while Tommy waited at the bar for the customers who never came, having a sip of beer every so often, although it was early even for him.

He straightened at the sound of someone entering the pub. A rare customer? Tommy greeted the pale, dark-haired young man, but straight away his gut instinct told him the fellow wasn't there for a drink. The guy looked very tough; not only did he have a lot of muscles, he had an edgy veneer, and intense, dark eyes, like he'd stab you just for giving him the wrong look.

Tommy's posture became more defensive as he waited for the guy to speak.

"Your name's Tommy?" he asked.

"Who wants to know?" Tommy asked, feeling for the gun he kept tucked into the back of his waistband ever since his mother was shot.

The guy seemed to sense what Tommy had hidden behind his back and held out his hands in a calming gesture of peace.

"I don't mean no harm," he said to Tommy. "I work with the Garcias."

Tommy knew he meant Johnny and Camille.

"You're really telling me they mean no fucking harm, after what they did to my mother?" Tommy said with a manic laugh, pulling out his gun.

"No, listen!" the guy shouted, panic in his eyes, looking like he was debating whether he had time to draw his own weapon. "It wasn't them, and I have proof. They hired someone, an invesligator, to track down who did it. It was your mother's drug supplier, he had her killed."

"That's not fucking proof, that's just your word," Tommy said, with his gun pointed at the guy. "This investigator, what's his name?" he asked, after a moment, figuring he might have heard of the person because of his work in law enforcement.

"It's some woman," the man replied, his voice sounding jumpy.

"Her name?" Tommy demanded.

"I think Johnny mentioned her last name's Fitzpatrick. She used to be a cop."

"Dana Fitzpatrick?" Tommy asked, barely able to control his shock.

Dana. So she *was* a private detective. Tommy hated her for going to their boss and spilling the secret he had trusted her with, but he also still had feelings for her despite her betrayal, something he would never admit to anyone. He despised Dana, but he still was attracted to her.

"She's really not a cop anymore?" Tommy asked the young man.

The guy seemed desperate to find the right answer to give to Tommy to please him but shrugged when he couldn't. "I don't know, I never met her. Johnny and Camille, they handled the whole thing."

So, Dana's life hadn't gone as planned either. Had she left the police because she missed him? Tommy wouldn't know unless he asked her, but he liked to think she had.

There was only one way to find out whether

this guy was telling the truth: ask Dana.

"Get the fuck out of here," Tommy told the guy, who rushed out the door.

Tommy realized the man had never told him his name and he hadn't asked for it.

He would have to ring Dana to find out the truth, and he wondered if he had her current number. She had reached out to him once over the past year, stopping by his apartment with immense pain in her eyes, but he had turned her away. It hadn't felt good hurting her, but then his pride was too great to give her forgiveness.

His grandmother would return soon, and he'd have to describe to her the events that had just unfolded. In the meantime, Tommy didn't need to look up Dana's number. He knew it by heart. He went to the phone and dialed.

He partly expected someone else, perhaps a new man in Dana's life, to answer. But, after a few rings, she answered, a voice he recognized immediately.

"Hello?" Dana said in her pleasant, warm tone.

"I didn't know if you'd changed your number," he said.

"Who is this?" Dana asked, her tone becoming more unsettled and annoyed.

"It's Tommy," he replied, a little stung she hadn't recognized his voice.

He heard her breath catch in her throat.

"Tommy, my God." She paused and seemed unsure about what she should say to him. It had been a year since they'd spoken. "How are you? I heard about your mother. I'm so sorry," she said.

"But you aren't sorry about costing me my job?" he responded sarcastically, then felt terrible for saying it, because he knew the words would break her heart.

"Tommy, I...I don't know what to say. I'm sorry I hurt you. At the time, I believed I was doing the right thing."

"And was it the right thing?" He knew he was making her feel uncomfortable by pushing her for an answer, but he genuinely wanted one.

"Tommy, you know I follow the rules."

"I know. You're a good girl," he said, with a grin that, of course, she couldn't see.

Dana laughed, and he'd missed hearing that sound, so he enjoyed the moment.

"I missed hearing you laugh," he told her.

"Why are you calling me, Tommy?" she asked him, as though she resisted returning his sentiment.

"I'm not looking for an apology from you," he replied, "although, it would be nice to get one."

"If I hadn't told them, Tommy, it would have put my career in jeopardy."

"But maybe I'd still have a career." He paused. "I heard you're no longer a cop," he said. "So we do have that in common now. Why did you stop being a cop? Was it because of me?"

"Don't flatter yourself," she said, and he could picture her smirking. "I had my reasons."

"Was one of them me?" he asked, hoping she'd left the police because she'd been devastated by what she'd done to him.

"Tommy, don't be cheeky, we aren't together

anymore. I don't owe you an explanation."

It was true. They weren't together anymore, and she didn't owe him anything, not even an explanation, but it would be nice if she gave him one.

"I heard you picked up some bad habits, Tommy," Dana said.

Tommy laughed it off. "I heard you know who killed my mother," he said to her after a moment.

"That's why you're calling me." She paused. "Tommy, I can't talk about my work with you," Dana said with a sigh. "You know better than to ask that. Who told you?"

"So, it's true, you do know who killed her. This guy who works for Johnny and Camille Garcia, the people who hired you, he told me."

"You should ask them," Dana replied.

"I can't trust them."

"But you trust me? After what I did?"

"Let's just say I trust you more than I trust them."

When she still wouldn't relent, he told her, "I don't think they'd mind if you told me. In fact, they would probably welcome it."

"They told you that, really?"

"No, but I basically told their enforcer that we knew each other. Dana, tell me. Do you want me to beg? 'Cause I will, if that's what it takes."

She sighed on the other end. "It was your mother's drug supplier. He ordered his men to kill her."

"Why? How can you be sure?"

"I have it on tape," she replied. "Be careful, Tommy, he wants to take over your neighborhood, and he wants your family and the Garcias out of the picture."

"How do you know that?"

"I just do. Okay? Goodbye, Tommy."

"Dana?" He wanted to say he still loved her but stopped himself. "Goodbye, Dana."

Tommy stood in place when she'd ended the call, holding the phone in his hand, as though he was unable to let go of it, unable to let go of her.

Finally, he put the phone back in its cradle and turned around when he heard his grandmother entering the pub. Tommy didn't need to see his grandmother to know she was there. It wasn't just that her presence was strong, she also always wore the same powerful, spicy perfume, named after a very addictive drug.

Catherine's arms were weighed down with shopping bags and Tommy rushed to help her.

"Did you buy out the whole shop?" he asked her jokingly.

His grandmother chuckled. "We've been short on supplies for the pub, so I thought I'd just buy everything at once."

"We have to be careful with spending money, you know that," Tommy chided her, lightly, because he knew her temper well, having been on the receiving end of it many times.

"If you reestablish your great-grandfather's business, then maybe we wouldn't be in the poor house," she responded in a not-very-subtle tone.

'Business' meant gangster business.

"We're not in the poor house," Tommy replied. Not yet, he thought, grimly. "Don't worry. I'll make sure everything is taken care of," he assured her, as he carried the bags and put them atop the bar to unpack.

"I know you will, sweetheart," she said.

"This guy came in while you were out," Tommy mentioned.

"And what did he want? I hope he wasn't causing trouble."

"No, nothing like that. He works for the Garcias."

Catherine suddenly looked worried.

"There was no trouble," he said. "The guy told me they know who shot my mother, that they have proof it wasn't them."

"Who are they claiming did it?"

"The guy who supplied my mother and Sam."

"The Swedish one?"

"Yeah, him."

"They could be lying," Catherine speculated.

"I don't think they are. Not this time, anyway. They hired a private investigator to find answers, and she was the one who told them about the Swede's involvement. I rang her, and she confirmed it."

"You don't know her, so how can we trust her?"

"I actually do know her."

Catherine gave him a look of surprise. "Who is she to you?" she asked.

"It's Dana Fitzpatrick, the woman who ratted me out."

"That cunt? You can't trust her."

"She isn't a cunt," Tommy said, suddenly very defensive of Dana.

"No, Tommy, she snitched on you. She's a fucking cunt."

"She thought she was doing the right thing."

"Did she apologize to you?"

"I don't want to talk about it," Tommy muttered, and his grandmother raised her eyebrows in a I-told-you-so way. "But she's telling the truth, I'm sure of it."

"You're really sure?"

Tommy nodded.

"You'd swear on your mother's memory?" Catherine asked.

"Don't ask me to do that," Tommy snapped at her.

Unfamiliar with being on the receiving end of his anger, she recoiled. "So, Sheila is right after all?" she said after a moment.

"It seems that way, yeah," Tommy replied.

"What's this Swede playing at, anyway?" Catherine mused aloud.

"Dana said something about him trying to take over the neighborhood, and that he wants us and the Garcias out of the picture."

"That fucker," Catherine said.

"I think I should ring Garcia, have a chat," Tommy suggested.

"Why? You want to work with them? Against that Swedish fuck? Your mother would kill you if she knew you were considering working with them."

"Unfortunately, I don't think we have much of a choice. It's not like she's here to object."

Catherine shook her head like she didn't

approve, but, for once, his grandmother didn't offer her opinion. She put away the groceries while Tommy called Johnny at his nightclub.

One of the large bouncers Johnny and Camille employed at the club answered the phone, but he seemed to already know who Tommy was, so Johnny must have been anticipating his call.

"I'll go get Johnny," the man told Tommy.

Tommy waited, with his grandmother eyeing him and gesturing, "What's taking so long?"

Tommy motioned for her to be patient.

"Tommy," Johnny said.

"I hear we got some business to talk about," Tommy told him. "Tell your friend thanks for stopping by."

"Henry? I hope he wasn't too rude."

"Nah, he was a perfect gentleman," Tommy spoke with sarcasm.

"Funny, he didn't say the same about you," Johnny said.

Tommy laughed.

"I just got off the phone with Dana Fitzpatrick," Johnny said. "She wanted to come clean to me about knowing you, before she worked any further for us."

"It's not her fault she told me, I basically gave her no choice," Tommy replied, not wanting to cost Dana the job. He didn't know her financial situation, but it couldn't have been easy for her to build a business from the ground up.

"You sound like you're in love with her," Johnny said bluntly.

Tommy didn't wish to get into a big discussion

with him about his intense history with Dana, so he said, "That Swede fucker already caused me trouble, and I hear he's gonna cause you trouble, too." He paused. "We should meet, to talk."

"Yeah," Johnny said, seeming agreeable to the idea.

"Just the two of us," Tommy said. "No henchmen. No women."

Johnny paused, then seemed to conclude, "I gotta bring Camille, or else she's not gonna be happy."

"Do you do everything your woman wants?" Tommy asked him, knowing he risked the other man's wrath by doing so.

"Camille's not just my wife, she's my business partner." Then Johnny seemed to comprehend that Tommy had insulted him. "You don't get to say nothing about my wife," he snapped at him.

Tommy would never admit it, but he could relate to Johnny, because he knew Catherine would insist on coming along with him.

"Take it easy," Tommy told him. "I didn't mean anything by it. My grandmother's gonna want to be there as well."

"I think these women are a little too involved in our lives," Johnny said with a chuckle, and Tommy laughed.

While Tommy couldn't imagine that he and Johnny would ever be friends, Johnny didn't seem like a bad guy.

Tommy knew Johnny would want to meet on his own territory, so before Johnny could pick the meeting place, Tommy quickly said, "Let's meet at the park near my pub. Can you be there in an hour?"

"Sure, we'll be there."

Catherine lingered nearby and rushed towards Tommy as soon as he hung up the phone.

"Tell me what happened," she said, staring at him.

"We're gonna meet them at the park in an hour," Tommy replied.

Tommy put the *Closed* sign in the window, and he and Catherine sat at the bar, watching the clock. Tommy had a beer while he waited, and Catherine, who rarely drank after becoming sober, sipped a coffee. Tommy smoked, which he had started doing after he'd kicked his heroin habit.

"Don't become too fond of the drink," she warned him. "I know stopping your drug habit hasn't been easy for you, especially with our family history of addiction. But don't turn to the drink. It's bad enough you smoke those damn cigarettes."

She meant his mother's history, of course, for she once had been an addict, too.

When they left to walk to the park, Tommy took his gun, just in case, and because he figured Johnny would have his.

CHAPTER SEVEN

———◆———

JOHNNY AND CAMILLE arrived at the park before Tommy and Catherine. Camille sat on a bench, while Johnny stood next to her, watching. Johnny saw Tommy walking methodically towards the meeting bench, looking around for signs that Johnny had broken their promise of not bringing any muscle. Johnny gave him a curt nod and Tommy nodded back.

Each seemed to be waiting for the other to speak first. Camille glared at Catherine, who stood to Tommy's left. Tommy was aware there was bad blood between Camille and Catherine, and that Catherine had even tried to shank Camille when they were in prison together. He didn't expect them to converse much during the meeting.

Then Camille said to her husband, "What the hell are we even doing here, meeting with these people? Do you know what she tried to do to me?" She pointed at Catherine. "She tried to fucking kill me, Johnny!"

"Yeah, I know," Johnny replied. "That was a while ago, baby. Let the past be in the past."

He seemed to be trying to calm his wife, but it wasn't working, and she kept glowering at Catherine, who, when Tommy glanced at her, had a fairly obvious smirk on her face.

"I don't expect you two to shake hands, but could you at least promise not to kill each other?" Tommy smiled.

While his dark good looks and charming smile seemed to appease most women—they certainly had worked on Dana—they had very little effect on Camille.

When neither of the women responded, Tommy nudged his grandmother's foot with his.

"I will, if she will," Catherine finally replied.

Camille stared blankly at them, then looked at Tommy and nodded.

"Good to know you ladies won't be ripping out each other's throats," he said to the women, with a wink at Camille, who either didn't notice or ignored him.

Johnny *did* see it, because he rose and said to Tommy, "Don't put the moves on my wife."

Tommy put up his hands in a gesture of peace. "I was only kidding."

"Yeah, you were," Johnny said, bluntly, as if Tommy wouldn't dare for it to have meant anything else.

Tommy knew that he had been slighted, but he couldn't go around attacking just anyone—even if he wanted to. That was the unique thing about Tommy, he didn't just have street smarts and toughness, he also had a sense for business, and years of experience dealing with difficult people and situations from his time as a policeman. He had a temper, but he could control it when it suited him.

"Mind if I sit?" Tommy asked Johnny, gesturing at the bench.

After a moment, Johnny nodded, and Tommy sat down. Then Johnny took a seat. Catherine and Camille took their places on either side of the men.

Catherine might have been tough—and pushy—but she knew her place, and so she let Tommy do the talking.

"Dana told me about our dilemma with the Swede," Tommy began the conversation. "It seems to me that he wants both of us out of the picture, so he can take over without any issues. Because he must figure, that if he takes out you, my family will take over. So he wants to rid the neighborhood of all of us, my family included, before we can cause him any problems. He wanted us to think you were behind my mother's death, so that we'd be distracted–or so that we'd all kill each other."

Johnny sat rigidly, seeming unsettled, as if Tommy could have a trick up his sleeve. At the same time, Tommy was thinking, is he hiding something?

"Yeah, I don't trust the bastard. I didn't trust him when I met him, and I sure as hell don't trust him now," Johnny said.

"You met with my mother's supplier? When?" Tommy sat tall and asked. "Why the hell would you do that?"

Catherine took notice of Tommy's suspicion and nudged his arm. Tommy motioned for her to wait.

"We met with him, sure, a while ago. Why wouldn't we?" Camille suddenly spoke to Tommy. "Your mother was dealing in our neighborhood. We never asked him to kill her."

"I can't fucking trust either of you," Tommy said, rising in anger, and he started to walk away. Then he wanted to turn around and beat the shit out of Johnny, but stopped when he realized his grandmother hadn't followed him.

She called him back, and Tommy wondered what was on her mind. It wasn't a secret that Catherine despised Camille, so why should his grandmother care if they walked away? But she seemed to comprehend the importance of an alliance, and Tommy considered that maybe she had a plan to use Camille and Johnny to get her family back in charge of the neighborhood rackets.

But Tommy wanted Camille and Johnny to know that he was in charge, not his grandmother. He took his time returning to the bench, and said to Johnny, "I'll stay, but the only reason I'm staying is because I want to."

Johnny nodded and Tommy watched him for a moment, then sat down next to Catherine.

"My wife mentioned you're close to Anton, who works for us," Johnny said to Tommy after a while.

"He dated my mother for a long time, and when I was a very young kid we were sort of close.

But that was years ago. Why, is there a problem?" Tommy asked, eyeing Johnny with mistrust.

"Dana didn't tell you?" Johnny said.

"Tell me what?" Tommy straightened his shoulders in alarm, as if Johnny was about to pounce at him.

"Anton is working with the Swede to destroy both of our families," Johnny told him.

"I don't believe you," Tommy said in anger, and started to rise again.

"Dana has him on tape!" Johnny shouted. "She's got proof."

But Tommy didn't look at him.

Catherine grabbed onto Tommy's sleeve, and he was forced to face them again.

"Dana has him on tape meeting with the Swede," Johnny said to him. "I can get her to play it for you, if you want."

Tommy didn't know Johnny well enough to trust that he wasn't lying, but Johnny had to have known that Tommy would end up confronting Anton anyway, and either way, he'd discover the truth.

"Anton has to be dealt with," Johnny said, bluntly.

Tommy had a very good idea of what he meant by 'dealt with', so he said, "I'll do it. I should be the one to do it."

Tommy still had a fondness for the man after all these years, and if Anton had betrayed his mother, he wanted to hear his confession himself.

CHAPTER EIGHT

BEFORE HIS MOTHER was killed, Tommy had sometimes stopped by the gentlemen's club Anton ran for the Russians, to say hello. It didn't hurt that there were plenty of beautiful girls there as well.

The morning after the meeting with Johnny and Camille, Tommy stopped by. He knew that the club didn't open until the afternoon, but that Anton would already be there, setting up for the day.

The tall, large man who guarded the entrance to the polished building knew Tommy's face, and so he was quickly allowed under the black awning and inside.

Inside the dim club, he found Anton standing by the bar, writing in a large book that probably had to do with the accounting for the place, and although it was early, there was a pint at his side. Tommy wondered if Anton still used drugs, as he vaguely remembered that being the reason his mother had kicked Anton out. Anton had been like a father to Tommy during the years when Tommy's real father was absent from his life, and then when Tommy's father died, Anton had been there for him. But that was many years ago, and Tommy had changed. He wasn't the same little boy who longed to be loved. The years had hardened him into a man who would do anything to succeed.

Tommy called Anton's name over the throbbing music, and he turned around.

"Tommy!" he said, greeting him as though Tommy didn't know the truth. And as far as Anton was concerned, Tommy didn't.

Anton only seemed to sense something was wrong when Tommy declined to shake his hand.

"Want a drink?" he said regardless, as though he wanted to sidestep Tommy's ominous mood.

A striking beauty in a bikini practiced her sultry moves on the dance floor under the soft lights, and Tommy's gaze drifted over her smooth, tan skin.

"I've basically known you my whole life, and I really want to give you the benefit of the doubt," he told Anton, looking him in the eye.

"Tommy, what are you talking about?"

"Anton, don't do this. If you really fucking care, then admit to me what you did. Because somebody's told me something about you, and it's not good. Don't just stand there and fucking lie to me. Give me the courtesy of telling me the truth."

Anton pushed the accounting book aside and gestured with his hands as if he had no idea what Tommy meant.

"I'm sorry about your mother," he finally said. "I know I haven't seen you since she died, but I always meant to give you my condolences."

"Your condolences?" Tommy said, not knowing whether he should laugh or scream. "Why the hell would I accept those from you, when you helped kill her?"

Anton's mouth hung open in shock, and Tommy didn't know whether he was a good actor, or if Johnny had lied to him.

"Who told you this about me?" Anton asked.

"Doesn't matter," Tommy replied, not wanting to give away the Garcias. "Anton, I've known you since forever. Tell me, is it true?"

Anton stood quietly, then asked Tommy to sit down at the bar. Tommy hesitated, then sat.

"I never actually hurt her," Anton told Tommy, not looking him in the eye, but at the bar.

"But you knew. You knew this whole fucking time who shot her and you never told me? You know I've been going mad looking for the guys who did it." Tommy slammed his fist on the bar, and a giant of a man exited the kitchen and stared at them.

Anton gestured at the man that everything was fine, and he went back into the kitchen.

"I cared about your mother," Anton told Tommy. "I loved her. But after she was killed, what was done was done. I knew I'd never win against that Swede."

"So you decided to fucking join him?" He paused, shaking his head. "All this time, I thought there was a man inside you, but now I know you're just a monster."

Anton held his hands to his face as though

he was genuinely distraught. "It's not personal, Tommy. I cared about your mother, and I care about you. It's business," he said, still unable to meet Tommy's forceful gaze.

"I appreciate your honesty," Tommy replied with sarcasm.

He started to rise, and Anton stopped him.

"What are you gonna do now that you know?" Anton asked him.

"I'm not sure," Tommy answered, but in his heart he knew what he must do.

Anton and the Swede had to die, and there was no way around it. That was what needed to be done to make things right, and even Anton himself must have realized that.

Tommy left the club, and went straight to his family's pub, where he rang Johnny, who agreed to meet him there.

Tommy's grandmother left the bar for upstairs when Johnny arrived, as Tommy wanted to be alone with him. They weren't scheduled to open for a few hours.

"Where's your wife?" Tommy asked him, not sarcastically.

"She doesn't always keep me on a leash," Johnny replied, with a smile, and Tommy chuckled.

It was a bit early for drinking, but Tommy gestured for Johnny to sit at the bar and offered him a drink.

"I don't drink much these days," Johnny told him. "But I'll take some coffee if you have that."

"Sure, we have it," Tommy replied, and went to pour Johnny a cup from the pot of coffee

Catherine had prepared that morning. "It's a little cold," he said, as he handed him the cup.

"I don't mind," Johnny said, taking a sip. "So, you said on the phone you believe me about Anton." He paused. "I'm surprised he admitted to it, the bastard—"

"Yeah, it seems he is a bastard," Tommy replied, not wanting to give Johnny too much time to gloat.

"What are you going to do about it?" Johnny asked, looking at him over his coffee cup.

Tommy was silent as he sat next to Johnny at the bar.

"Have you killed anyone?" Tommy asked him.

"Sure. Haven't you?"

Tommy shrugged. He had, of course, but he didn't want Johnny to know his secrets. When he'd killed his mother's boyfriend Sam, no one outside the family knew. Still didn't. There was Sam's family, of course, who had come looking for answers, but he and his grandmother had managed to brush them off. For now. Being a former police officer had been helpful in that instance. When Tommy had discovered that Sam was going to betray his mother by making a deal with the police over their drug business, Tommy had to stop him.

Tommy knew that Johnny expected him to kill Anton. But Tommy didn't plan to kill Anton himself. It wasn't that he dreaded it since they'd been close when Tommy was younger—he would be able to overcome that—Tommy wanted Johnny to prove his loyalty in their partnership. He

wanted to know he could trust him with anything, and what better way to prove that than
murder?

"You're going to kill Anton," Tommy told him,
casually.

Johnny paused, then said, "I don't take orders
from nobody." He sounded calm, but he clenched
his cup in his hand.

"They aren't orders," Tommy replied. "I need
to know I can trust you."

"You don't want to do it yourself, so you're trying to make me do it," Johnny said, setting down
his cup so forcefully some of the coffee spilled
out of the saucer onto the bar.

"That's bullshit," Tommy said. "I have no problem killing that fucking bastard myself. But we
need to seal this partnership of ours somehow."
He paused. "Besides, Anton works for you, so he's
really your problem."

Johnny chuckled at Tommy's reasoning. "You've
given me no choice," he said. Then he watched
Tommy carefully. "But, I don't take orders from
no one."

"I know that," Tommy replied, wanting their
partnership to continue. For a second, he thought
Johnny would rise and storm out of the place,
or try to beat the shit out of him, but Tommy
was confident he would win in a fight. Johnny
remained seated, touching his hand to his chin, as
if he was thinking.

"I'll do it, I'll kill the fucking bastard. But you
fucking owe me for this."

"And I'm sure you won't let me forget that," Tommy said with a grin.

CHAPTER NINE

A FEW DAYS AFTER Tommy met with Johnny, he rang Johnny for news, and when Johnny didn't return his call, Tommy decided to pay a visit to his house in the suburbs.

Tommy never really ventured outside of the city much, and he had only been to the suburbs a few times in his life, but as he drove he watched the landscape change from the hard surfaces of gritty concrete and brick buildings and scrubby weeds and trees to more lush leafy scenery. Here the trees towered above the roadway offering dappled shade that cooled the surroundings. He found it almost mesmerizing as it was so far removed from what he knew.

Johnny had never told Tommy where he and Camille lived, so Tommy had asked a friend from his police days for the address, knowing very well he risked Johnny's wrath by showing up unannounced at his home, but he was eager for news.

When he arrived at the house, how quickly he found a place to park on the street amused him. In the city it would have taken him a lot longer. He walked away from his car, giving it a parting glance. Did it fit in in this neighborhood? Not really. It wasn't a piece of shit, but most of the cars parked by the houses here were luxury models. Tommy frowned, then continued on his way. Maybe someday he'd be able to afford a nicer car.

Johnny and Camille lived in a beautiful white brick house with large colorful gardens in the front, side, and back yards, complete with a flowing two-tiered fountain in the front garden. There was also a huge attached garage for what he assumed were their numerous expensive cars. They had done well for themselves over the years, though Tommy knew their earlier lives had been the opposite of wealthy.

Tommy rang the doorbell and somewhat expected Johnny to pull a gun on him when he answered, but much to his surprise, a beautiful young woman came to the door.

"Are you the babysitter for the Garcias?" Tommy asked her with a wink.

The dark-haired girl half-laughed at him, but her lovely brown eyes were shy and kind.

"I'm their daughter," she said, brushing a strand of her long hair out of her eyes.

Tommy's mouth almost hung open. The last time he had seen their daughter in the neighborhood, she had been a child. Now, she was a gorgeous woman.

"I'm Tommy," he said, reaching to shake her hand. "What's your name?" He smiled.

"Phoebe," she replied, accepting his handshake.

He wanted to find out her age but didn't want to come across as too forward to Johnny's daughter. "Is your father home?" he asked instead.

"My dad's home."

Tommy heard Johnny shouting, "Phoebe, who are you talking to?"

"Tommy," Phoebe called to her father over her shoulder.

Johnny raced to the door and moved Phoebe aside. "What the hell are you doing coming to my house?" he questioned.

"Relax, I come in peace," Tommy said with a grin, holding out his hands to show Johnny that he didn't have a weapon.

Johnny frowned. "You shouldn't come to my home without asking me first."

"I tried reaching you, but you never returned my call."

"I've been busy."

"I hope you have been," Tommy replied, and Johnny gave him a knowing smile, then a look that conveyed he didn't wish to discuss business matters in front of his daughter.

Tommy wasn't surprised that Johnny wanted to keep his daughter safe from the brutal realties of the crime business, and if he'd had a daughter, he'd want the same thing for her.

"Can I some inside?" Tommy asked. "I promise I won't bite," he added, and Phoebe giggled.

Johnny gave her a look to be quiet. He seemed reluctant to let Tommy into his home, then he glanced at Phoebe and motioned for her to go upstairs, and Tommy averted his gaze from her nice backside as she walked away and up the stairs.

"You have some news for me?" Tommy asked

Johnny once he was inside the house.

Johnny gestured for him to enter the kitchen.

"My wife went shopping," Johnny said as he sat down at the table and motioned for Tommy to sit.

It was clear to him that Johnny wouldn't offer him coffee, that he wanted Tommy to leave as soon as possible. He risked Johnny's fury by asking, "Is your daughter still in school?"

Johnny shook his head. "She already graduated." He paused, then looked at Tommy closely. "Why are you asking me about my Phoebe?"

"No reason, I just remember her from the neighborhood. She's a lot older now."

"She's nineteen, she's still a young girl," Johnny replied, as though to make it clear to Tommy that Phoebe was off limits—to him, and if he had his way, to every other man as well.

"Yeah, she is, of course," Tommy said in agreement, although he was very much attracted to her.

"I don't even let her date yet," Johnny said with a chuckle.

"I can see why," Tommy murmured.

"What's that mean?" He gave him an angry look.

"I didn't mean nothing by it," Tommy said to calm him.

Johnny grinned. "I scared you, didn't I?" he said with a laugh. "I know, she's beautiful, she takes after her mother. But don't ever tell Camille I said that."

"Why? Wouldn't she be happy?"

"Phoebe's my daughter from another woman," Johnny explained. "Camille and me took her in when her mother died years ago."

"I'm sorry, I didn't know that."

"Not a lot of people do. Camille treats her as her own."

Sympathy for Phoebe filled Tommy's heart. He had lost his father when he was just a child.

Then Johnny appeared eager to change the subject. "I'm sure you came here for news about what we discussed," he told Tommy.

"I'm listening," Tommy replied.

Johnny rose to check that Phoebe was out of earshot, then he sat down again.

"I took care of it," he told Tommy.

Tommy had been fond of Anton as a boy, and his heart was heavy for a moment. Then he thought about what happened to his mother and he found strength. He waited for Johnny to say more, and when Johnny didn't elaborate, he said, "I'm gonna need a few details."

It had been Tommy's great grandfather's trademark as a gangster to leave a body part of whomever he killed, usually a finger, at a place in his neighborhood where it would be found by others, as a warning to anyone who might even consider betraying him. Tommy had never asked questions when his mother told him this, as it had frightened him as a boy. Now, he thought it was grim, but he could also appreciate his great grandfather's brutality.

"I didn't take anything from him," Johnny replied. "I was going to, then I thought to myself, what if the police catch me with whatever I take? They can use it as evidence. I got rid of the body. I can't tell you how, but I can tell you that it won't be found."

"You want me to take your word for it?" Tommy asked him, internally debating whether he believed him.

Johnny nodded. "You're gonna have to, if we're gonna work together. You're gonna just have to trust me."

Tommy sat there quietly, thinking. Johnny was right, of course, but Tommy didn't know him that well, and he never trusted those he didn't know.

"You know, your wife's family and mine have never really got along," he said. "So, as you can imagine, it's hard for me to take your word for anything."

"I'm being honest, I promise," Johnny said, and the sincerity in his eyes convinced Tommy to believe him, although he still planned to be cautious.

"I trust you," Tommy told him, untruthfully, and they shook hands, as their gazes met. Neither man took his eyes off the other for a moment, then both stood, and Johnny went with Tommy to see him out of the house.

To Tommy's surprise, Phoebe waited near the front door.

"How long have you been standing there?" Johnny asked her, seeming more than a little alarmed.

"Don't worry, I just came down a second ago. I didn't hear anything," she said with a knowing smile, and Tommy grasped that she knew enough about her parents' 'business'. She gave Tommy a flirtatious look. "You're leaving already?" she asked him.

"Yeah, your father and I were just talking business," he said, fighting his attraction to her in front of Johnny's watchful gaze. He was normally much more brazen with women whom he found attractive, but he was very aware how protective Johnny was of his daughter.

"Business," Phoebe said with a flirty smirk, and with her soulful brown eyes brightening, "that's an interesting way to describe it."

Her sarcasm only increased his attraction to her, but he resisted giving her a smile in front of her father.

Johnny cleared his throat, which Tommy took to mean he should leave, but he gave her a wink on his way out when Johnny wasn't looking.

CHAPTER TEN

THAT TOMMY CERTAINLY was handsome, but Phoebe knew her father's associates were off limits to her. That didn't mean she would stop thinking about him. She had sensed a past between Tommy and her father, or maybe between her stepmother and Tommy. She wasn't sure which.

The day after she met Tommy, she stopped by her parents' house again, but they weren't home. Phoebe had a housekey, so she went inside.

Sometimes, she wished she had a sibling, but her parents didn't speak about why she didn't have one, and Phoebe sensed there was sadness behind the reason, so she didn't ask them about it.

She entered the kitchen, made a cup of tea, and sat at the table to drink it.

She knew both her father and stepmother weren't perfect, but she'd always been curious about Camille's life, because she hadn't been told that much about it. She internally debated whether she should act on her instinct to have a look at Camille's things. Maybe she'd find out more about Tommy from them.

Phoebe quickly finished her tea, then she went upstairs to her parents' bedroom, a place she hardly had entered throughout her time living at home. Overcome by a sense of guilt, she paused at the doorway. But her desire to discover something about Tommy propelled her to enter. Nobody was home except for her, but, still feeling guilty, she closed the door behind her, as though that made what she was doing a little more forgivable in her eyes.

She turned her attention to the space at her stepmother's side of the bed, where Camille kept a lovely, decorated wooden box on a small table. Was it locked? Phoebe opened the box carefully, wondering what it held inside.

She found what looked like a journal or a diary inside. Camille didn't seem like the kind of person who kept a journal, so surprise filled Phoebe's head.

What did it contain? Camille's life story? Perhaps something about her parents' connection to Tommy?

There wasn't a lock or even a clasp to keep it shut, so Phoebe was able to immediately open it. She didn't know when her parents would return or how much time she had, so she raced through the pages. Camille seemed to have started the journal a few years ago, and the most recent entry was about Billy, who had helped rescue Phoebe from Vito and Marie Russo. Billy seemed to have been a former boyfriend of Camille's, which Phoebe hadn't known. She'd thought they were just friends. According to what Camille wrote,

Billy had died recently, and that shocked Phoebe, because she didn't recall her stepmother mentioning it. Although she did remember a period a few months ago where Camille had acted downtrodden. In her journal, Camille didn't say how Billy died, just that he had passed on. The news filled Phoebe's heart with despair. After all, Billy had helped save her and had driven her father to the hospital after Marie shot him. Phoebe wanted to offer her sympathy to Camille, as she had sensed the connection between the pair, but she knew that doing so would reveal she had secretly read the journal.

What Phoebe saw on the next page made her hands shake, and she nearly dropped the book.

On the pages Camille had expressed absolute fear for Phoebe's safety during the time Phoebe was being held by Vito and Marie, and her concerns were genuine, from what Camille's words revealed about what Vito had done to her as a girl, something no woman should ever have to endure.

The journal fell out of Phoebe's hands and landed on the soft carpet. She felt absolutely shaken, because what Vito had done to Camille could have happened to her.

Then anger overcame her, and more than ever, she wanted revenge. Not just for herself, but also for Camille. Vito had tried to hurt Camille by targeting Phoebe, and now Phoebe would do the same to him. So what if it was Vito's daughter Marie who had kidnapped her? Vito must have known something about it, even though he had acted surprised when Marie rushed into their home with the abducted Phoebe. Against her parents' wishes, Phoebe would go after Marie. But she wouldn't be able to do it on her own. She would need help. Who could help her? Who *would* help her?

Tommy. She didn't know him well, or hardly at all, really. But the moment she met him, she felt as if she could trust him, there was such sincerity in his eyes.

Phoebe picked up the journal from the floor and quickly put it away.

CHAPTER ELEVEN

TOMMY HAD JUST finished setting up for the day when he heard the pub door open. He looked up from the bar, wondering who it could be, and hoping it wasn't someone unpleasant. But what he saw in front of him, who he saw in front of him, was very pleasant. She was absolutely lovely.

The beautiful, dark-haired Phoebe Garcia, Camille and Johnny's daughter, had entered the pub. She seemed timid in the small space, or maybe she just didn't go out to drink that much and felt inexperienced once inside the pub.

"Phoebe?" he said with a smile. "What are you doing here?" Had she come to deliver a message from her father?

Tommy's grandmother was in the upstairs area of the pub, and she came down to see who had arrived.

"You look lost, sweetheart," she said to Phoebe, giving the shy girl a smile.

"I'm here to see Tommy," Phoebe replied, glancing at him.

"You two know each other?" Catherine asked,

looking surprised. She didn't appear to recognize Phoebe. She gave Tommy a look that conveyed disappointment. She probably thought Phoebe was one of Tommy's many conquests and didn't approve of the girl's young age.

Phoebe looked at Tommy for what to say, and Tommy replied to his grandmother, "This is Johnny and Camille's daughter. We met the other day."

Catherine became friendlier, offering the girl a place to sit down and asking if she'd like a drink. Again, Phoebe looked to Tommy for what to do. She seemed to want to speak with him alone, so Tommy told his grandmother, "I'll take care of her."

Catherine hesitated, then moved to the farther end of the room, sat at one of the tables, and began reading a magazine.

Tommy motioned for Phoebe to sit at the bar.

"I don't think I should offer you a drink," he said with a wink.

"I'm old enough," Phoebe replied.

"Yeah, but I don't think your father would like it much. What's going on?" Tommy asked her, and she had that look about her again, as though she was lost. "I don't think you came here to ask me out on a date." He smiled.

Phoebe blushed and turned her head away.

"Do you want a Coke?" he asked her.

Phoebe shrugged, and he found her uncertainty endearing.

Her gave her a Coke anyway and smiled to himself when she drank it.

"I was right, you did want one," he said. "How did you know where to find me?"

"It wasn't easy," Phoebe said with a sigh. "But after you visited my dad, I knew you were probably in this neighborhood because my parents control it."

So, she was aware of what her parents did for a living, and Tommy felt relief that he wouldn't have to hide that from her.

"I asked around, carefully, so my parents wouldn't find out," Phoebe told him. "Most people wouldn't talk to me because they're afraid of upsetting my father. But one person did, and that led me to this place. And here I am."

"I'm a lucky man," Tommy said with a grin. "Why are you worried about your parents finding out you came here?" He figured that Phoebe must have wanted something from him that would displease them.

"I need your help," she said, meeting his gaze, and his attraction to her strengthened.

"What do you need my help for, sweetheart? You hardly know me," Tommy said with a smile.

"I know you must be a gangster," she replied.

"How do you know that?" he asked her.

"Because you hang around with my dad."

"You're just a child," he told her, dismissively, feeling his grandmother watching them.

"I'm nineteen," she replied with determination.

Except for Catherine's presence, they had the place to themselves, as was often the case these days.

"All right," he said, leaning across the bar and

looking at her. "What do you need?"

Phoebe brushed a loose lock of her soft, dark hair out of her eyes, in a way that was so tender, he wanted to kiss her. Then she told him, calmly, "I want to get revenge."

For a moment, he wondered if she was joking, then her saw the solemnity in her eyes.

"Against who?" he asked her, standing up. "Why does someone as innocent as you want revenge?"

"I just do. Okay? And I need your help."

"Why not ask your father for help?" Tommy replied after a moment.

Phoebe shook her head. "He won't help me. My stepmother won't either."

"Why not?" Tommy asked.

"They think it's too dangerous."

"Who's the person you want revenge against? They must be very powerful if they frighten the likes of your family."

Phoebe turned away as if she wouldn't tell him.

He touched her arm lightly. "Phoebe?"

She looked at his hand on her arm, then at him. "Marie Russo. She's Vito Russo's daughter."

Tommy pulled his hand off her. "Vito fucking Russo's daughter?" he said, taking a step back behind the bar.

Phoebe nodded, as though unfazed. "You're gonna help me or no?"

"Russo's in the fucking mafia," Tommy replied. "Going against him means I lose my balls, or worse."

"You're not man enough? I'm a girl, I need your help."

"You're a very pretty girl," he told her. "You seem like a sweetheart. I'd like to help you—"

"Don't try to let me down easy," she cut him short.

Tommy glanced at his grandmother, who was watching them with curiosity.

"Why do you want revenge against them?" he asked, attracted to her and wanting to help her, but undecided about what he should do.

"It's his daughter who I hate," Phoebe answered. "A few months ago, she kidnapped me, and her father was a part of that."

Tommy shook his head in disgust. "That's terrible, I didn't know that happened to you."

"There's a history between my stepmother and Vito, and his daughter blamed my stepmother for her father falling on hard times. Vito, he hurt my stepmother, badly, when she was just a girl. He's not a good guy."

Tommy sensed that 'badly' meant an assault. Suddenly, he felt very protective of Phoebe. "Did he hurt you 'badly'?" he asked.

Relief surged through him when she shook her head.

"Russo's got quite the reputation," he said, after a moment.

"Yeah, that's why my parents won't touch him or his family, and they don't want me to do anything either."

Tears formed in Phoebe's eyes, and Tommy saw just how deep her pain went. He reached to touch her face. "I don't like seeing you cry."

"What do you care if I cry?" she replied,

between sobs, as his fingers slid across her soft skin. "You're not going to help me. What happens to me isn't your problem." Her body shook with her crying and she wouldn't meet his gaze. "No one wants to help me."

Tommy sighed, his hands damp from her tears. "I want to help you, Phoebe, I just don't know how to do so without starting a war with the Italians, a war I can't win," he told her with honesty.

"I thought you were different," she said, then rose as if to flee.

"Phoebe," he said, reaching for her. "You hardly know me."

"Your eyes seem trustworthy," she told him, and he smiled at her innocence.

"I want to help you," he emphasized.

"But you can't," she finished the sentence for him.

"I don't know," Tommy said, in frustration, more to himself than to her. "I need to think."

Phoebe nodded.

Tommy gave her a wistful smile. "I trust you'll come looking for me."

She didn't return his smile, then quietly left, and Tommy was crushed that he'd disappointed her.

As soon as the Phoebe was gone, Catherine went over to him and demanded to know what had happened.

"What the hell does the Garcia daughter want with you? You aren't fucking her, are you?" his grandmother scolded.

"No, she's too young," Tommy said. "She wants

my help with something."

Catherine stood there, giving him a stern look, and Tommy knew she wouldn't leave it alone unless he told her everything.

"Stay away from her," his grandmother advised upon hearing the whole story.

Wanting to make his own decision, and wanting to help Phoebe, Tommy shrugged off the advice.

Catherine grabbed him by the shoulders as best as she could given his height. "Tommy, I mean it," she told him, staring up at his face. "She'll only cause you, *us*, trouble."

"I can't promise you I will," Tommy replied, and he could see in his grandmother's eyes how his harsh honesty had seared her heart.

CHAPTER TWELVE

D ANA SAT IN her car outside a café that the Swede frequented in the city with some of his gang. She had the engine off.

She had continued to keep an eye on the Swede for Johnny and Camille. Anger flushed her face as she sat there, watching him, with his callous smirk and sinister eyes, chuckling at something one of his thugs had said as the group of men sized up their young, blonde waitress salaciously, and one of them reached out to slap her backside. The girl gave them a startled look, then hurried away.

After a few moments, Dana's attention drifted to the warm afternoon scene on the street, the couples walking together, enjoying the sunshine, the groups of teenagers laughing with each other as they passed by her car, and a few women carrying shopping bags out of the stores that advertised steep discounts on their windows.

When she turned her attention back to the men inside the café, they had vanished.

Someone knocked loudly on her window, and she looked up and saw the Swede standing there, grinning, with his two men at his side.

He motioned for her to roll down her window, and she panicked about what she should do. She didn't have a weapon on her, but she was very certain he did. She considered starting the engine and speeding off, but worried he would shoot at her car, possibly striking her.

She decided she would pretend she didn't know who they were.

"Yeah?" she said, opening her window only a little.

"You've been following me," he replied, still smiling. He indicated a gun hidden at his side. "We can do this the easy way, or the hard way," he told her. "You fucked with Anton, you fucking bitch?" he said to her, not raising his voice, staying eerily calm and in control.

"I don't know who you are or what you're talking about," Dana said. "Get out of here before I call the police." She knew she risked his wrath by saying that, but was desperate for him to leave.

Dana started to close the window, but he banged his fist against the glass.

"Do what I say," he told her, "and I won't fucking shoot you right here."

Trying to pacify him, Dana held her hands in a gesture of surrender. She considered telling him she had been a policewoman, but that could endanger her life even more.

"Get out of the car. Now!" he ordered.

Dana glanced at the locked door, then at him, debating what to do. She reached for her clunky mobile phone, a new luxury she had given herself for her business. The Swede looked at the phone and shook his head, gesturing with his gun.

Dana's hand slowly crept away from the phone. She unlocked the car door and opened it. She knew she might not get out of this alive. It was late afternoon and still light, but nobody was paying any attention to what was going on at Dana's car. Everyone was too busy going about their own business—shopping, rushing to eat, meeting up with friends—all the normal routines people busied themselves with, unlike those who had to tail dangerous criminals for a living. Dana sighed and stepped out onto the street, and with his two beefy thugs at his side, the Swede ordered her into a large black SUV parked nearby, concealing the gun just enough so that nobody on the street could see it. But she could.

She felt as though she was walking towards her death, and she might have been, for all she knew.

Dana stopped before she stepped up into the car. "Where are we going?" she asked him apprehensively. She considered screaming for help, but knew they would shoot her if she did.

"You'll find out," he scoffed. Then he shoved her inside the car and slammed the door closed.

Dana tumbled onto the seat and took in her surroundings. The dark interior. The tinted windows. The fact that she knew the doors were locked but she didn't see any door locks.

One of the thugs, the taller, younger one, climbed into the driver's seat, while the Swede sat down in the passenger seat.

Then the door at Dana's side swung open, and the other thug pushed his way into the backseat with her. Dana recoiled, wondering what he'd do to her.

He stared at her for a moment and chuckled at her fear. The car started and he shouted at her to put her hands out in front of her. Dana hesitated, then complied when he continued giving her a menacing stare. He roughly fastened a piece of robe around her wrists and ordered her not to move.

"Where are we going?" she asked him.

"Shut up or I'll give you something to put in that pretty mouth of yours," he said, and the sin-ister glimmer in his eyes made her shudder with dread.

"What the hell is going on back there?" the Swede asked from the passenger seat.

"This bitch won't shut her fucking mouth," the man next to her answered.

"You'll have to train her," the guy driving said with a laugh.

"Assholes," Dana mumbled to herself.

The man next to her nudged her sharply with his elbow, and she winced.

"What did you say, bitch?" he asked.

Dana wanted to spit in his face, but instead she did nothing. "I didn't say anything," she replied, hoping he would leave her alone and internally dreading his reaction.

He pretended like he would strike her, and chuckled when she flinched. She turned away from him, hoping he would forget about her. A moment passed and he remained silent, and she let out a faint sigh of relief.

Dana tried to decipher where they were taking her, although it was difficult for her to see anything through the darkened windows. One of the men in the front seats switched on the radio and pulsating nightclub music filled the space, and her mind filled with horror upon realizing they were truly in control.

Dana knew she had to do something, anything, to change the situation, no matter if it put her life in danger, because she might not make it out alive, regardless.

She waited until the car stopped at a red light and the man seated next to her was distracted chatting about his girlfriend's breasts with the Swede and the other man in the front row. Then she raised her bound hands and hit the window, desperate for someone outside to notice.

"What the fuck are you doing, you crazy cunt?" the man alongside her shouted, twisting in his seat to grab her arms. "This bitch is causing trouble," he said to the men at the front. "She's pounding on the fucking window."

"Doesn't matter," the Swede answered indifferently. "No one's gonna hear her." He muttered something to himself, and the other man with him chuckled.

"What are you going to do with me?" Dana demanded.

"Whatever the hell we want to do," the man at her side replied smugly. "Ain't that right?" he asked the Swede, who shrugged.

Although outwardly he seemed less vulgar than the men with him, it was his calm demeanor that chilled Dana more so than the others frightened her. She couldn't tell what he might do, and that alarmed her greatly. From her days as a police detective, she knew that such behavior warranted even more caution.

"Put the blindfold on her," commanded the Swede.

The burly man next to Dana covered her eyes with a dark blindfold and fastened it tightly around her head. The car drove on for about another thirty minutes or so and then came to a stop. The man next to her stayed with her, while the two other men exited the car. Then the door near Dana opened and someone pulled her outside, where she landed unsteadily on her feet. Enveloped by darkness, Dana tried to listen for clues as to where she was. She could hear traffic in the distance and the sounds of water nearby. A breeze caressed her face, giving her a moment of pleasure and contradicting her situation in a cruel way.

The Swede ordered her to move. She recognized his voice despite not being able to see.

"Take your time," he told her, in his odd, calm manner. "We wouldn't want you to fall and hurt yourself." The false sincerity in his voice infuriated Dana.

"What do you care what happens to me?" she snapped at him.

"You could be a good bargaining chip," the man who had been seated with her—she recognized his voice—replied.

They made her wait and stay still for a moment,

and she heard a door being opened. Then they ordered her to walk forwards.

"Slowly," the Swede emphasized.

Everything will be okay. Everything will be okay. Desperate to cling to hope, Dana repeated the words in her head, like a prayer.

She almost tripped going up a step and walked through what must have been a doorway and entered a cold room, and then she heard a door slammed shut and bolted behind her.

One of the men shoved her from behind, forcing her to walk forwards. She heard what sounded like another door closing, then one of them grabbed her and turned her around.

"Sit," the Swede said.

Dana slowly felt with the back of her legs for something to sit on and sat down on what felt like an uncomfortable wooden chair. She could feel them grabbing her arms and tying them, and then her legs, to it.

Rough hands touched her face in a hard, indifferent manner, then suddenly she was able to see again. The blindfold had been removed.

Dana quickly absorbed her surroundings. She was seated inside a dim, windowless room in what appeared to be a warehouse.

"What is this place?" she asked the Swede, standing in front of her, with an unreadable expression.

"It's what I call my office," he replied, and she understood him to mean his headquarters.

One of them grabbed her shoulder from behind and squeezed her hard. She tried not to show pain but flinched.

"What's the matter?" the man, the youngest of the three, asked her. "Afraid?"

He chuckled when she stayed quiet as her body quaked under his grasp.

The Swede flicked a switch and a bright light shone down on her from above, casting a glare in her eyes. Dana squinted.

"You used to be a cop, right?" the Swede asked her.

She didn't answer him, but her eyes must have given her away, because he said, "I knew it. I can smell cops a mile away. Who paid you to spy on me? You had something to do with Anton going missing?" he asked her.

"I know nothing about that," she replied, calmly, trying to shrug off the other man's hand still on her. "Honestly."

He continued to rest it on her shoulder despite her resistance.

The third man exited the room for a moment, and Dana could see a sliver of light in the hallway, as if he'd opened the door to another room and turned on the light. He returned a little while later with a long, serrated blade, and handed it to the Swede, who grinned as he stared at it in his hands.

He held the blade under Dana's chin, and she recoiled and held her breath. Her body became absolutely still.

"You're gonna tell me everything you know, or else I'm gonna use this to ruin your pretty face," he said, in a restrained voice, despite the fire in his eyes and the reddening of his skin. "Then I'm gonna make sure my guys each get a chance to fuck you before I slit your throat, bitch. Slowly."

The coldness and cruelty in his eyes, and his sinister smile, made her quiver, because she could tell he very much meant what he'd said.

Dana started to scream, hoping someone, anyone, outside might hear her. The three men looked at each other and chuckled.

"You can scream all you want, sweetheart, nobody's gonna hear you," the Swede told her, moving the blade down to between her breasts.

CHAPTER THIRTEEN

—————◆—————

TOMMY STARED AT the half-empty bottle of whiskey on the coffee table in front of the couch where he sat. It seemed to stare back at him, challenging him to have another drink. Just one more.

He had tried not to think about his mother and the fact that she was gone, but it had very much affected him today, and so he started drinking, and once he'd started, he couldn't stop.

Tommy wasn't a mother's boy, but without a father, she'd been the one to raise him, with his grandmother's help, and they'd been very close.

The urge to drink was overcome by an urge for something that would take him completely away from the earth, at least for a few moments. He hadn't used heroin in a while, but he suddenly wanted to. Badly.

The reason he'd stopped using drugs in the first place was because he knew his addiction would have devastated his mother, who had also been an addict in her youth, but recovered. Now, with his mother gone, did it really matter? His grandmother would despise him for it, but they didn't have the close bond like he'd shared with his mother, and so her disappointment wouldn't affect him in the same way.

Tommy picked up his phone to ring the guy who'd been his dealer, then stopped himself after dialing the number partway. He set the phone down on the table, grabbing it a moment later, and dialing Dana. She didn't owe him words of comfort, but he wanted to hear her voice, and the first thing he thought of when he thought of comfort, was Dana's warm, rich voice. She didn't answer. Where was she? Still at work? With another man? The thought of her being with someone else caused him to clench his fists.

He desperately wanted to hear her voice again and, intoxicated, wasn't thinking right, so he recalled the number Johnny gave him and rang her at work.

A man with a youngish voice, answered. "Hello?"

"Who is this?" Tommy said, more loudly than he'd wanted to.

"This is Brian, Dana's assistant," the guy said.

"Oh," Tommy muttered, feeling a bit foolish. "Is Dana there? Let me talk to her."

"She's not here at the moment. Can I ask who's calling?"

"Tommy," he replied. "She knows me."

"Tommy, right," Brain said, as if Dana had mentioned him.

"When will she return? It's important that I speak with her soon."

"I'm not sure. She should've returned by now."

"Where did she go?"

"Uh," Brian sounded hesitant to divulge that information.

"Dana's talked about me to you, hasn't she? So you must know I used to be a cop. You can tell me where she went."

"There's this guy," Brian said, then paused. "She's being paid to watch him," he continued after a second. "He's Swedish or something."

"Fuck," Tommy said as he thought of what Johnny had done to Anton, and how livid the Swede must have been now that his friend had vanished.

"Should I go to the police?" Brian asked, seeming alarmed by Tommy's reaction.

"No, I'll handle it," Tommy quickly replied.

"Are you sure? What are you going to do?"

"I can't tell you. Trust me."

"I'm sorry, but I don't know you," Brian replied.

"You don't, but trust me when I tell you, this is the best way to ensure Dana's safety."

From his years in law enforcement, Tommy knew that police involvement could cause the Swede and his crew to panic and endanger Dana's life.

"I don't really have a choice, do I?" Brian said.

"No, you don't," Tommy told him bluntly. "I promise you I'll make sure she returns unharmed."

"Are you saying you know where she is, that someone took her?" Concern filled Brian's voice.

"I have a pretty good idea who has her, yeah."

"I don't like the sound of that. I—"

"I have to go now, Brian, there isn't time to

chat," Tommy said, and when Brian started to interrupt him, Tommy continued, firmly telling him, "*Don't* call the police."

Tommy had to sober up. Fast. He took a quick, cold shower, then made coffee in the kitchen. His head pounded as he drank the hot, bitter liquid, forcing two cups down. Feeling better, he rang Johnny to explain his predicament.

When Johnny sounded reluctant to become involved, Tommy said, "The reason this happened to Dana is because she's working for you," trying to appeal to what little conscience Johnny might have.

"Just a second," Johnny replied, then it sounded like he'd covered the phone and seemed to be talking to someone else. Camille, probably.

Tommy waited.

"Camille wants me to stay out of it," he told Tommy after a moment.

That selfish bitch, Tommy thought to himself. Of course, he couldn't say that to Johnny.

He decided to appeal to Johnny in the only way that could definitely work—by questioning his manhood.

"Do you do everything your woman says?" he asked Johnny, taunting him just enough to hopefully get him to reconsider.

Johnny's reaction could go either way: it could make Johnny change his mind, or he could tell Tommy to go fuck himself and hang up the phone.

"What the fuck, Tommy?"

"I'm just saying, it seems like your woman's got

you by the balls if she's telling you where you can and where you can't go."

"She doesn't tell me to do nothing," Johnny snapped at him. Then he paused and drew a breath.

Knowing that his plan was working, Tommy smiled to himself.

Johnny spoke again after a minute. "I'll fucking help you."

"Ain't that what friends are for?" Tommy said, with a sparkle in his voice.

They agreed to meet outside Tommy's apartment. Tommy waited for Johnny by his living room window that overlooked the dark street dotted only with one or two faint lights. A few cars sped past, and then Tommy saw two people walking by, laughing loudly.

Johnny had mentioned something about bringing guns. Lots of them. Tommy hurried and got his handgun from his closet and tucked it into the small of his back, under his shirt. It was his lucky gun, it had belonged to his father, and even if Johnny brought more powerful ones along with him, he wanted to have it on him.

After what felt like a long time, Tommy spotted a car arriving. It took him a moment to recognize Johnny in the driver's seat of the quiet, ordinary-looking car. Johnny parked outside on the street, and Tommy put on his leather jacket and hurried downstairs.

Johnny opened the car window when he saw Tommy approach him, and said, "Hop in so we can get going." Tommy nodded quickly to Johnny, who was wearing a hat, and Tommy could hear Spanish music being played at a low volume on the car radio.

"Nice car," Tommy joked. "I almost didn't recognize you."

Johnny chuckled. "We'll need to blend in," he said as Tommy opened the passenger door and entered the car.

"I know you know where this fuck who has Dana lives," Tommy told him quietly, in case someone was listening.

"Yeah, you don't have to give me directions," Johnny replied.

Tommy's large frame filled the compact space.

"You're too fucking big for my car," Johnny said in jest.

Tommy chuckled a little, but he wasn't in the mood for a joke. His body felt genuinely like ice as he thought of what could be happening to Dana right then, what they could be doing to her. He could hardly think of anything else. Then rage filled his veins and he told Johnny to drive.

"I got so many fucking guns in the back that you won't believe it," Johnny mentioned, matter-of-factly.

"I can believe it," Tommy said. "Does Camille know what you're doing?" he asked out of curiosity.

Johnny shrugged. "She knows what she needs to know."

Tommy seemed to have hit a nerve with Johnny, who changed the radio station and turned up the volume and focused on driving. Tommy listened to the pop music on and off, but it irritated him. He needed to concentrate and wanted silence. After a few minutes, he couldn't take it any longer, and shut off the radio.

"What the fuck did you do that for?" Johnny said.

"I don't like the noise," Tommy said casually. "You're lucky I didn't break the fucking thing."

At that, Johnny started laughing. "You're fucking crazy, do you know that?"

"Yeah, I know it," Tommy said dryly, not in the mood to have a laugh.

He focused on the window, at the dark scenery that flashed by as they rode, which was flecked with the lights of the restaurants along the sidewalks and the cars around them. Someone cut in front of them, and Johnny swerved, but didn't beep the horn or chase them. The last thing they needed was to be stopped by the police with all those guns in their car.

Johnny left the main street for a side road, which took them to an isolated area surrounded by neglected former factories, and he turned off the car lights as they drove farther in. They didn't have a plan, exactly. Tommy got the feeling that Johnny didn't think much of making plans.

Suddenly, Johnny stopped the car, and propelled Tommy back into reality. The engine quieted. Johnny started to say something, then tapped Tommy's arm.

"That's the building," he said, pointing at a nondescript structure about twenty yards away in the night.

Then lights shone on the car from behind as another vehicle approached.

"Who the hell is that?" Johnny said.

Since they were blocking the way, the other car had to stop, and someone exited.

"What the fuck?" Tommy said, and reached for his gun.

"It's a fucking pizza deliveryman," Johnny said, then chuckled in relief.

The guy, a baby-face teenager, approached Johnny's window. "What the fuck do we do?" he asked Tommy. "I'm not gonna kill some fucking kid."

The boy gestured for them to move their car, and Tommy asked Johnny for some money.

"What the hell do you need that for?" Johnny replied.

Tommy ignored him and asked again, and Johnny relented, handing him a large bill.

Tommy got out of the car. He now had a plan.

The delivery boy, who seemed flustered, asked for Tommy to move the car, and Tommy attempted to smooth things over.

"Where are you delivering to?" he asked the kid, who gestured to the building they had in their sights, the Swede's headquarters.

"Can you move your car?" the boy asked, again. "The food's going to get cold and I won't get a tip."

"You deliver to these guys a lot?"

The boy nodded, seeming surprised that Tommy knew who they were.

"You know them?" he asked Tommy.

Tommy replied, "You could say that." He took the money out of his pocket. "I'm gonna give you this and you're gonna give me the pizza and go away."

The boy looked at the money and smiled, then he seemed to think of something problematic and stared at Tommy. "What am I going to do with the other pizzas? There's more than one."

"Throw them out the window, I don't give a shit," Tommy said, shoving the money into the kid's hand. "Just get the hell out of here, and you didn't see us. The last part's very important. You understand?" Tommy looked him in the eye.

The kid seemed to sense what Tommy meant, that Tommy would find him and kill him if he told anyone what happened.

The boy went to his car and handed Tommy a pizza. "Give me your hat," Tommy said.

"What?"

"Just give it to me."

"I can't. The owner will dock my pay if I come back without part of my uniform," the boy whined. Tommy took the hat off the deliver boy's head and thrust another couple of large bills into his hand.

"That should take of it. Get out of here. Now!"

The pizza guy drove away, and Johnny got out of the car.

He gestured to the pizza Tommy was holding. "What the fuck are you doing with that? What the hell is going on, Tommy?"

"I got a plan," he replied. "I'm gonna deliver this fucking pizza to them. It's dark, they can't see nothing out here, they can't see my face, not with me wearing this hat. That's how we get them to open the door. Then you know what we're gonna do next. Get the guns."

Johnny removed a small machine gun from the back of the car.

"Check out this beauty." He showed Tommy the weapon. "Of course, none of this shit is legal," he said with a smile, and Tommy chuckled.

Tommy reached for the gun. "I'm taking this one."

"You already got your own."

"I know, but I like this one better."

"You're fucking crazy." Johnny shook his head and smiled.

"I know." Tommy said. And it was the truth.

CHAPTER FOURTEEN

A S SHE SAT tied to the chair in the dank, dark room, Dana found it hard to breathe with her mouth covered and a clogged nose from allergies that seem to have gotten worse since she was forcibly taken. She hadn't a clue about where she was, and what little she could hear in the distance didn't make her location obvious.

She heard the two burly thugs who the Swede had left in charge of watching her, speaking to one another outside the door, and fear filled her mind as she anticipated them entering the room to hurt her again. The first time had been awful enough, the way they'd touched her in her most intimate places as she trembled in fear and tried in desperation to stop them, but couldn't. As a former policewoman, she was a very tough person, and to be put in a position where she was entirely vulnerable had nearly destroyed her soul. She feared what they would do to her next, that it would be even worse.

She wondered where the Swedish one had gone to. Not that the Swede, the bastard that he was, would stop them from hurting her.

Someone knocked in the distance, and Dana heard the sounds of a door being opened in the distance. Thinking that somebody had come to the building's front door, possibly the police, she tried to scream, but the sound was muffled. She moved furiously in the chair, trying to make as much noise as possible. Sweat dripped down her entire body.

Then she heard silence. Thinking that whoever had come had already left and that she'd never get out of this alive, Dana started to sob, and struggled to breathe with the weight of her agony.

Then she heard gunshots, the sound of objects falling and men shouting, and, right then, everything changed as a warm rush of hope filled her veins.

She moved in the chair she was tied to, and could do so only a few inches at a time, with her feet tied together to the chair, trying to make herself heard over the noise by slamming the chair legs down onto the floor.

Then she heard footsteps running down the hallway outside the door of the room where she was being held, and someone began to push in the door from the other side. She started to make the chair go up and down more, as far as she could, making as much noise as possible. Thinking that she was either being rescued—or it might be her end—she closed her eyes tightly, not wanting to see the events play out.

She heard the sound of more than one person entering, and someone touched her shoulder, firmly, but in a way that it comforted her.

"You're safe now," the calm, deep, voice assured her, and before she opened her eyes, she knew it was him.

Tommy.

She opened her eyes, and saw his handsome face standing in front of her, and, immediately, she felt safe again. He gently removed the covering from her mouth.

"Tommy, what are you doing here? How did you know where I was?" she asked him as she breathed out, in a haze of relief that she'd been found, and no longer had the urgency to flee. Then she saw Johnny standing behind him and knew how Tommy had found her.

Tommy quickly undid the ropes and Dana leapt up from the chair and embraced him. He stroked her hair lightly, as if he was unsure how she'd feel about him touching her.

"I love you, Tommy," she told him. "I'm so sorry I betrayed you."

He let her hold him, but was quiet, and Dana wondered what that meant. Did he not feel the same way? Had he found someone else? It wasn't too long ago when he'd been so heartbroken, but she didn't know what had transpired between that time and now. But something had changed.

Johnny touched Tommy's shoulder. "We need to get out of here."

Dana stepped back from Tommy's embrace and followed them, with their guns drawn, outside the room, staying near Tommy's side as she went.

Dana stopped walking and drew in a sharp breath when they reached the entranceway at the sight of the two guards who had brutalized her now dead on the floor. Blood flowed freely from the wounds on their heads where they'd been shot. As a former policewoman, Dana had strong morals, but she wasn't displeased to see them there like that after what they'd done to her.

Tommy gestured for her to continue to follow them and Dana shook her head, unable to move from where she stood.

"What's wrong?" Johnny asked.

Dana turned to Tommy and whispered, "They hurt me", not wishing to reveal her secret to both men.

"What do you mean?" Tommy asked her, with a look of fire in his eyes.

Dana gestured at the men. "They did things to me—unspeakable things—when he—the one in charge left."

Tommy's face reddened and his body shook with fury. He demanded to know what exactly she meant, but Johnny urged them to leave before the Swede returned.

They left the building, entered Johnny's car, and as they drove away, Dana could breathe with ease once more.

CHAPTER FIFTEEN

A FTER RESCUING DANA, Tommy and
Johnny took her to her place, where her
assistant Brian waited for them. Tommy had
convinced her to not involve the police in the
matter, which, secretly, he planned to take into
his own hands. After he and Johnny had parted,
Tommy returned home, the Swede and how
Tommy would have to do something about him
soon heavy on his mind.

The next day, he was woken very early by
someone knocking on his door. Tommy grabbed
his gun from his bedside and put on his jeans.
Knowing very well that it could be someone
unpleasant, Tommy demanded to know who was
there through the door.

"It's Phoebe," the sweet, soft voice replied.

He answered the door, shirtless. "You're one
person I wouldn't mind seeing," he said with a
smile.

She ignored his flirting and pushed her way
past him inside the apartment.

"How do you know where I live?" he asked
her cheekily as he closed the door. "I don't think

I ever told you."

"If you must know, I followed you home the other day," she told him, defiantly, standing close to him, although she only reached his chest.

She stared at his body for a moment, then quickly looked away, and her innocence charmed him.

"Put a shirt on," she told him, still unable to look at him.

Tommy chuckled, then grabbed the shirt he had placed on a chair and put it on. Phoebe glanced in his direction, saw he was dressed, and finally looked at him again.

"What did you come here for? Hoping I might kiss you?" Tommy asked with a smile, and Phoebe rolled her eyes.

"You know why I'm here," she told him, "I'm here for an answer."

"About?" Tommy acted as though he didn't understand her, when he very much did. He just wanted to avoid giving her the answer she sought.

"You know, Vito Russo and his daughter, Marie."

Tommy didn't know what to tell her. He liked her and didn't want to chase her away, but he didn't want to agree to something that could end terribly for him.

He suddenly felt tired. The events of the past twenty-four hours had been so draining. He sat down on the couch and put his hand to his face.

"What's wrong?" Phoebe asked him, sweetly, sitting down next to him.

"Nothing, I'm tired," he mumbled.

Phoebe rose. "I'll make you coffee. Where's your kitchen?"

He pointed her in the right direction and listened in case she needed help.

"Find everything?" he called out to her.

"Yes," she replied, out of his view.

Tommy listened to the sounds of Phoebe making him coffee, and after a few minutes, he could smell the fresh aroma.

"How do you take it? she asked

"Neat—black, no sugar."

Phoebe emerged with a cup and handed it to him gently.

Tommy took the warm cup from her and smiled. "You're a real sweetheart, thanks."

"Funny how I came here wanting something from you, and now I'm gonna sit and listen to your troubles," she said, sitting down next to him.

"You are?"

Phoebe nodded.

"So, what's wrong?" she asked him, after giving him a little time to drink his coffee.

"I had a bad night," he replied.

"You drank too much?"

Tommy shook his head. "I had to help someone who was being hurt by these fucking horrible people. I had to help someone I'm close to."

"A woman?" Phoebe asked him. Out of jealousy or curiosity? Tommy couldn't tell.

Tommy looked into Phoebe's pretty dark eyes and nodded.

"Is she someone special to you?" Phoebe asked, pretending to be uninterested, but Tommy sensed she very much wanted to know.

Tommy wasn't sure how to answer her question. What was Dana to him now? He cared for her, and she seemed to care for him, and he still felt affection towards her, but the feelings he had now didn't have the same intensity as they had in the past. Tommy knew then that, while he was fond of Dana, he wasn't in love with her.

"She was, a long time ago," he answered.

"Not anymore?"

"Not anymore." Tommy stared at Phoebe thoughtfully. She was very young, but also very beautiful with her soft-looking, full lips.

"How did you help her?" Phoebe asked after a moment, quietly.

"Do you really want to know? Because I don't think you do. In fact, I don't think I should tell you," he said with a smile.

"Why not? You're afraid I can't keep a secret?" Phoebe replied, giving him a rare, dazzling smile.

"You don't smile enough," he commented. "You're even more beautiful when you do."

"Even more?" Then Phoebe looked away from him. "You really think I'm beautiful?" she asked quietly.

"You're the most beautiful girl I've ever seen," he said with honesty.

She looked him straight in the eye. "I bet you tell every girl that."

Her confidence propelled him to grab her lightly by her wrist. "I don't tell every girl that, just you."

He stared directly at her, and, sensing his sincerity, she melted into submission. Tommy wrapped her in his arms and held her close, kissing her, softly at first, and then with more force.

Phoebe put her hand on his chest and stopped him, with a look of shame in her eyes.

"What's wrong?" he asked her.

"You know my father won't like this."

"You think I'm afraid of him?"

Phoebe suddenly looked panicked. "Don't hurt him, he's my father!"

Tommy touched her arm to snap her out of her state. "Relax, I'm not going to do anything to him."

"You're not?"

Tommy shook his head and chuckled. "Do I really frighten you that much? How come you kissed me, then?"

"I like you," Phoebe said. "A lot," she added shyly, not looking at him.

"Your father, he doesn't scare me, but I respect him. Okay?"

"Okay," Phoebe said faintly, touching his hand, and her skin felt soft and warm against his.

Feeling a change of heart, Tommy suddenly pulled his hand away from hers. "You're too young."

"I'm nineteen," she insisted, touching the front of his jeans.

Tommy moved her hand off him. "Your father would kill me if he found out."

"Not if you killed him first," Phoebe said, and gave him a serious look. Then she let out a peal of laughter. "Just kidding." But a darkness deepened her eyes and caused his attraction to her to strengthen. Women who had a sinister side, like himself, were irresistible to him.

"I want to hear about how you rescued this girl," Phoebe said to him, seeming to give up on seducing him, at least for the moment.

Internally, he debated whether he should tell her, but her beauty got the best of him, and Tommy looked at her lovely face, and told her about the men he killed last night, leaving out the part about her father's involvement, of course.

Tommy expected her to be shocked by his confession, but she sat there calmly, seeming to reflect on how she should reply.

"You're not frightened?" he asked her, finding her charm even more alluring.

"Of you?"

"Of what I did," he replied.

Phoebe shook her head. "It's justified. You did it to protect a woman you care about."

Tommy gave her a smile. "You'll make some man a good wife someday."

"Some man? But not you?"

"We'll see," Tommy said, with a grin.

"So, are you going to give me what I want?"

Tommy gave her a gentle pat on the face. "Phoebe, you're a sweetheart, but you know I can't go after Vito Russo. You know if I go after the mafia, I'm a fucking dead man. But, since you are such a sweetheart, maybe I can do something about his daughter."

Phoebe's expression darkened. "You better help me, or else I might tell my father you hurt me."

Tommy stood up and shook his finger at her in anger. "Hurt you? Phoebe, you wouldn't…Why are you saying that?"

"I'm desperate, that's why. Can't you see that? And if you won't help me, you *are* hurting me."

"I'd never fucking hurt you. I said I was gonna help you. You're a crazy girl." He stared down at her, shaking his head.

Phoebe was quiet for a moment. "I know, I'm sorry," she said, gazing up at him, her eyes widening with guilt.

"So don't say shit like that ever again. I mean it." The partnership Tommy had formed with Phoebe's family was vital, and he couldn't let anything jeopardize it.

Phoebe looked up at him innocently and nodded. "What are you going to do to his daughter? What are you going to do to Marie?"

"How much do you know about her?" Tommy asked, sitting down again.

Phoebe shrugged. "Not much. I followed her a couple of times. She works in a beauty shop."

"She owns the shop?"

"I think so."

Tommy was silent for a few moments as he thought.

"Tell me what's on your mind," Phoebe interrupted, unable to wait even a short time for an answer.

Tommy made her wait a little longer because he liked the eagerness in her eyes, then he said, "Like I said, I ain't going after Russo himself, but I can do something to his daughter's shop."

Phoebe grabbed his arm and held on, and when Tommy looked at her, he could tell he had her completely enthralled. "What are you going to do to her shop?" she asked him, her eyes widening in awe.

"I know someone, a specialist, from when I used to be…" he stopped short of saying, *a policeman*.

Phoebe nudged him, and he said, "I know someone who'll take care of it."

Internally, Tommy reasoned that Marie probably had insurance, but it would keep Phoebe happy, without creating a massive problem for him.

Phoebe crawled into his lap and put her arms around his neck. "Thank you. Thank you," she said as she began to kiss his face.

Tommy gently pushed her off him and shook his head. "Phoebe, don't."

"Why not?" She gave him a wounded stare.

"You know why." He paused. "Listen, I'll help you out because I promised, but please leave my home. Now," he said, loudly.

She glared at him, then stormed out, slamming the door as she went.

Her anger only magnified his attraction to her. Tommy took a moment to settle down, then picked up the phone to ring his contact to arrange what he'd promised.

CHAPTER SIXTEEN

THE NEXT DAY, Dana rang Tommy and asked him to meet her at the coffee shop near his home.

Dana got there shortly after him, and he waved at her when she didn't notice him upon entering. She smiled and went to his table. He had waited for her arrival before ordering.

"How are you?" Tommy asked her, with genuine concern, as she sat down across from him.

"I'm still a little shaken, but I'll be fine," she replied, giving him a faint smile.

"I've been worried about you," he said, reaching for her hand, but brushing past hers as she pulled away.

"Tommy, please don't. Please don't make me believe you have feelings, too, when that's not the case. I…"

He struggled to hear her over the noise of the morning crowd. She hadn't said on the phone why she wanted to meet him or what she wanted to discuss, and Tommy wondered if he'd have to break her heart by telling her he wasn't in love with her anymore.

A server stopped at their table and they ordered coffee. Tommy asked him to not add milk to both of theirs, as he knew that was the way Dana also liked to drink hers.

"You remembered how I like my coffee," Dana said to him with a nostalgic smile.

"I do know you very well," Tommy replied, a little sadly.

"You do," she said.

"What's going on?" he asked her, after a moment. "Why did you want to see me?"

He'd been a little worried that something had happened to her again.

"Has someone threatened you?" Tommy asked.

He knew the Swede was still out there, and the thought that the man might go after Dana again disturbed him.

"No, nothing like that has happened," Dana replied, not meeting his gaze, and he could tell something wasn't right.

"Dana, what's the matter?" he asked, a bit more loudly, her secrecy causing a mix of anger and fear inside him.

"Nothing's wrong. I just wanted to thank you, Tommy. Why are you being so paranoid?"

That caused him to snap. "Why am I being paranoid? Because you were kidnapped and almost fucking killed, that's why." He couldn't control his voice, and the people seated around them began to stare.

"Find something fucking else to look at!" Tommy shouted at them.

Dana told him to calm down. "What's going on

with you?" she asked him when he settled.

Telling her the truth would make him look soft, so he lied to her and said, "I don't know."

But he did know. Very much. He wanted the Swede dead for what the man had done to her and to his mother, and he knew that while he wasn't in love with Dana anymore that almost losing her had nearly driven him to madness, because even though she'd hurt him, he still cared about her.

"Tommy, I wanted to thank you." She paused, glanced at the table, then at him. "I love you, Tommy. I'm so sorry about what I did, how I betrayed you." Tears shone in her eyes.

Tommy hesitated to speak, and in silence, Dana reached across the table and patted his hand, seeming to sense he didn't reciprocate her feelings, and as if to reassure him she was okay with that.

Relief filled Tommy's mind. "I still care about you, and I can forgive you. But I don't feel the same way anymore."

"I know," Dana replied, quietly, giving him a sad smile. "I can accept that, but I don't want to."

"So, in that case, what do we do?" he asked her with a slight smile. "Are we friends?"

Dana looked away and shook her head. "No, Tommy, I can't be friends with you."

"I'd like to keep in touch," Tommy countered.

"You can count on me if you need something, but don't expect us to be hanging out regularly," she said, meeting his gaze, a glimmer of defiance in her eyes.

"I can accept that, Dana. But I want to stay in touch, hear how you're getting on."

"Knowing how you feel, it won't be easy for me to keep you in my life, but you did save me, so I do owe you for that, at least." She gave him a wistful smile.

They finished their coffee, and as they were leaving, after Tommy insisted on paying, Dana touched his arm and said, "You know, I've been thinking about the Swede."

"You shouldn't think about that bastard," Tommy told her with concern.

"I can't help it. After all, I used to be a detective and I watched him very closely for the Garcias. Anyway, I've been thinking and doing some research, and I have this theory." She paused, as if she was concerned that he would dismiss her.

"What is it?" Tommy asked, because he was curious.

"I've given a lot of thought to this, so please hear me out." Dana paused and looked around cautiously. "I think he could be bringing in his drugs through the garbage barges." She waited a moment and looked at Tommy as if to gauge how he might react. Tommy was silent and his face seemed emotionless.

"Here's what I think. They leave the harbor loaded with trash, right? Practically overflowing most of the time. When they come back to port, they're empty. Only, maybe they're not. Maybe, on the return trip they're loaded with drugs that they picked up from a boat or some kind of watercraft that was waiting for them to make the handoff. The drugs could be hidden somewhere inside the barge, where they can't be seen, at least not easily. That way, he keeps everything under the radar."

Tommy considered her idea for a few moments, then said, his eyes brightening, "It sounds crazy, but you could be right. How did you come up with that?"

"I was standing on the pier, not far from the docks, just looking out at the water, trying to relax a bit and I noticed the comings and goings of several rubbish barges—they move pretty slowly, so, even though they're a distance from the shore, with binoculars I could see them well enough."

"You take binoculars to relax by the water?"

Dana seemed a bit taken aback for a moment. "So, maybe I like to look for shore birds. You don't know everything about me anymore. I find I like to bird watch sometimes. It makes a nice change of pace from everything else."

Tommy thought about that for a bit. And he also thought about how he could use what she said about the barges to his advantage.

CHAPTER SEVENTEEN

———◆———

MARIE RUSSO STOOD helplessly in front of what remained of her beauty shop, now a smoldering pile of ash. She had raced over as soon as the man who owned a neighboring shop phoned her with the terrible news, but she had arrived too late, and the shop was already engulfed in flames.

Smoke stung her throat and made her eyes water as she watched the firemen extinguish what remained of the blaze.

Marie hadn't called her father yet. She'd been too distracted while waiting for the firemen to finish, troubled about what might have happened to the keepsakes that had been inside her shop. What had become of them? Were they safe? They were framed autographed photos of her mother Isabella with famous people she had met through Vito's mafia connections. Isabella had been a naïve girl newly arrived from Portugal when she succumbed to the charms of the older and more experienced Vito with his mob lifestyle and flashy cars, and the gifts of jewelry he gave her. She fell in love with him but they never married. Marie was the result of their relationship and when Isabella became pregnant, Vito helped take care of Marie.

Marie lived with Isabella until she had to return to Italy. Marie had been in sporadic contact with her father over the years but when Isabella left the country, around the time Camille's mother divorced him, Marie went to live with Vito and took his surname. The pictures that hung on the shop's walls were irreplaceable. Marie had arrived too late to risk entering the shop to grab them. How would she tell her mother? Isabella had written a week ago that she was coming back, and Marie had promised she would keep the pictures secure.

But then she remembered something else.

Desperate to move quickly and find out, she pushed to the front of the crowd that had gathered to watch. The firemen had escorted her away from the building when they arrived right before her.

But now, one of the firemen, his face covered in soot, saw her approaching and shouted at her to come speak with him and another man who stood near him. Marie hesitated. Something didn't feel right. Why did he want to talk with her when they hadn't wanted her near them at all before?

As she stepped closer, she saw that he held something in his hand, and when she comprehended what it was, she had difficulty standing and nearly fainted.

It wasn't one of her mother's photographs.

In his hand, the man had a parcel of the cocaine she'd been hiding in the shop's basement. One parcel of many that had been inside, which she had been holding for a man called the Swede, without her father's knowledge, for a large sum. Marie had a little gambling problem that her father didn't know about, and the Swede had offered her a way to take care of it.

What transpired next felt like a very bad dream to Marie, who remained frozen rather than flee. She could have gone to her father, but she feared his anger and his disappointment in her more than she feared being arrested. The fireman had already radioed the police, who arrived quickly and seemed to judge her at once when they saw her standing there with the firemen.

An older man who looked like a detective, wearing a suit and polished shoes, approached her as the other policemen began to search the remnants of her shop for evidence of more cocaine.

The detective grabbed the parcel from the fireman. "Is this yours?" he asked Marie.

She debated how to answer, and spent time thinking about the outcomes of each answer.

"It's not mine," she finally said.

The detective clearly didn't believe her. "It isn't yours, but it was inside your shop?"

"Somebody made me put it there."

"Your father? I know who your family is, Ms. Russo."

"It isn't his."

"I don't believe you." He paused. "We're going to keep looking, and I bet we'll find a lot more where that came from."

Marie tried to conceal her fear as she spoke with him. What if the Swede's spies saw her with the police?

"Have a look," Marie said, trying to sound nonchalant. "You won't find anything." She was confident the other parcels had been destroyed in the fire.

Marie stood in the cold while the detective and police searched the scorched remains of her building. She hadn't worn a coat when she left her home, and since they were now treating her like a criminal, no one had offered her a blanket.

The police had brought bright lights with them to shine on the scene as they worked, and they had set up a barrier to keep away the crowd. After a while, she heard them shouting excitedly and she knew they had found something.

"Fuck," Marie muttered under her breath.

The detective approached her triumphantly, carrying two more parcels of the coke. "These aren't yours?"

"Bastard," Marie said faintly so that he wouldn't hear.

Marie began to panic. She still feared her father finding out more than she feared the Swede, and once her father heard about the fire, he would be on his way to her. She quickly explained that she was holding the drugs for someone, that they didn't belong to her.

He listened to her, and then replied, "It's still a crime."

"I know," Marie said, "but the only reason I

kept it for this guy is because I feared he would kill me if I refused."

That part was a lie, as Marie very much knew what she was doing. Yes, she had somewhat helped the Swede out of fear when he approached her, but also the money was very good.

Marie was a pretty woman, with a beautiful smile, and she tried her best to win the detective over. Growing up in a world of tough, manly men who mostly ignored their women unless they were sleeping with them, Marie had learned early on to use her looks to get what she wanted in life.

"Can you help me, please? I'm terrified!" she pleaded.

"Can't your father help you?"

Marie shook her head. "He doesn't know, and he'll kill me if he finds out."

"Really, your own father?"

Marie nodded. "You don't know him like I do, but surely you know of his brutal reputation?"

"Brutal to his own daughter?"

"He doesn't make exceptions," Marie replied, when, in reality, she was her father's little sweetheart, but he'd kill her if he knew she had betrayed him by working with a competitor, as he would do to anyone else. "Help me and I'll help you. I'll tell you anything you want to know about this man these drugs belong to."

"You expect me to just let you go?"

"No, but I'm trying to appeal to your good nature. I'm sure you're a smart, kind, reasonable man. You seem that way to me. Anyway, I'm asking you to not arrest me here, in case the drug dealer's spies are nearby."

At that idea, the detective peered around the area, and Marie couldn't tell if was trying to humor her, or if he thought that the Swede's men being in the area was a genuine possibility.

"Go home," he told her.

Marie looked at him as though he might be playing a trick on her.

"Go home and wait, and one of us will stop by in an unmarked van to take you somewhere safe where we can chat."

"How do you know I won't just run away?"

"Because if you do, I'll personally tell your father what you've been up to." The detective winked at her.

Marie could see that he was serious and felt her skin flushing. She gulped and agreed to his plan.

"Come quick," she told him. "My father will find out what's happened and rush over to my home."

The detective assured her she wouldn't have to wait for too long.

Marie could feel the detective's gaze on her as she made her way past the crowd and returned home, where she changed her clothes and waited by the window for the unmarked van to arrive. After a while had gone by, and no one came, she paced back and forth in her living room, dreading her father's probable arrival before she could leave. And, once the police got there, how would she explain the van waiting outside to him? Vito wasn't a fool and would know that something was amiss.

What looked like a delivery van slowly pulled up in front of her home and parked. The white van had a large red rose painted on its side.

Marie's heart skipped a beat as thoughts of the Swede and his men being inside the flower delivery van, tricking her, raced through her mind. But she had to get out of there now, if she didn't want her father to find her.

Marie grabbed her purse, exited, and hurried down the front steps. A man in a delivery uniform stepped out of the van and approached her on the sidewalk. Uncertain about whether she could trust him, Marie paused, and when she caught a glimpse of the police badge he held covertly in his hand, she resumed walking.

He opened the door, ushered her inside the van, then quickly shut the door.

Marie had expected the interior of the police van to look like they did on television, but inside it just looked like a plain van.

A woman sat quietly in one of the seats, and it was difficult for Marie to see her face clearly in the poor light, but she did notice the woman's red hair, tied back and up away from her face.

"Marie," the woman said in a voice that sounded slightly deep for her, with warm, rich undertones.

"Who the hell are you?" Marie snapped as she settled into her seat.

"I'm Detective Everhart," the woman answered, in a calm tone.

True, she did look like a detective, with her bulky suit and imposing demeanor.

"Where the fuck are you taking me?" Marie demanded to know.

"Relax," Detective Everhart said, gesturing with her hands.

"No, I will not fucking relax until you tell me where we're going!"

"We're taking you some place safe to talk. Nothing sinister is happening."

"I want to see your face better," Marie replied.

"Why?"

"So I can see if you're lying."

"There's not much light in here, sorry," the detective said casually.

Marie thought for a moment about whether the detective's answer satisfied her, then looked away resolutely, and crossed her arms. She could feel the detective deriding her posturing.

"Is something funny?" she asked, looking Everhart in the eye.

The detective stared directly at her and shook her head. Marie sensed she had finally met her match, but she would never admit that aloud.

Marie once again turned her attention away from the detective. There were no windows so there was nothing to look at outside the van. After a moment, something unpleasant occurred to her. The man driving had shown her his badge before she entered the van, but what if it had been fake and the Swede had sent them to find her?

"Are you going to kill me?" she asked Everhart, or the woman she knew as Everhart, anyway.

"Why would you think that?" Everhart chuckled.

"You would know why if you knew the guy whose drugs these are."

"You have nothing to worry about, Ms. Russo."

Still, Marie wondered.

They spent the remainder of the drive in silence, with Marie focusing on the comforting rhythm of the moving vehicle, and after what seemed like a long time to Marie, the van stopped in front of a simple brick home.

"What's happening?" she asked Everhart.

"We've reached our destination."

Marie could hear the driver exiting the van and approaching the door at her side. She began to get up, but Detective Everhart gestured for her to wait.

"Where the hell are we?" Marie demanded.

"You'll find out soon," Everhart replied.

The door at Marie's side slid open, and the man who had been driving stood outside, waiting to help her get out.

Outside, Marie could see the building clearly, and it looked like an apartment complex rather than a single home.

"What the hell is this place?" she asked the man.

Detective Everhart, who had heard her, edged close to Marie and answered, "You'll be safe here."

"How long will I be here?" Marie asked, panicking a little. "I didn't bring my suitcase."

"Don't worry," the detective replied, in a surprisingly warm tone. "We have things you can use."

Still unsure, Marie nodded uncertainly. Once

they ushered her partway inside the dim building, the weight of everything Marie had been through over the past few hours began to sink in and exhaust her, and despite having a strong spirit, it was a struggle for her not to cry.

Who had started the fire at her beauty shop? Marie's father had many enemies, and so did Marie because of him. But Marie had a feeling that *she* was the intended target. And who had every reason to despise her? That little bitch Phoebe Garcia. Marie doubted Phoebe was capable of starting the fire on her own, so someone must have helped her. Who? Camille?

Detective Everhart's hand hovered near Marie's shoulder for a moment, then vanished when Marie moved away abruptly to deflect the kind gesture.

Marie quickly regained her composure, and they resumed leading her inside, through a long, badly lit hallway into a large, dim, room with a few comfortable-looking chairs and a television. Marie's gaze focused on the dark curtains covering the windows. Then she turned her attention to a man seated across from where she stood. His face seemed familiar to her, and she recognized him as the detective who had been at the scene of the fire.

"I've kept my word, Marie, I've kept you safe. Are you going to keep yours?" he spoke to her. "I'd like you to talk with Detective Everhart and tell her what you know."

"I'm hungry," Marie said, glancing at the rays of light sneaking through a space in the curtains.

"It's nearly morning, and I haven't had anything to drink, either." She paused. "I'm not saying nothing until I get something to eat and drink."

He gestured at the male policeman and tasked him with the job of getting her food and water.

"I don't want water," Marie interrupted. "I want a coffee."

The detective glared at her for a moment, then told the policeman, "And get her a coffee."

Marie smiled to herself as he hurriedly left the building.

"Let's go somewhere so we can talk," Detective Everhart spoke to her.

Marie didn't look at her but remained focused on the male detective.

"I'm not saying anything until I get my food," she told him.

"You really are your gangster daddy's spoiled brat, aren't you?" He smirked.

"Fuck you!" Marie shouted and spat in his direction. She moved to attack him, but Everhart grabbed her from behind and restrained her.

"Calm down, we're trying to help you," she told Marie.

Marie thought of her mother's photographs that had been destroyed in the fire and became emotional. She shook her head in exhaustion. What the hell was she doing here with the police? She could tell them everything she knew about the Swede but then they'd abandon her, leave her alone to deal with his wrath. She didn't know who she could trust. From a young age, her father had instilled in her the belief that the police weren't to be trusted. Ever.

"You're gonna help me, really?" she questioned Detective Everhart. "I'm gonna spill my fucking guts to you and you're not gonna throw me to the wolves!"

Everhart looked at Marie and smiled. "We're not going to do that. Let's go in the other room to start talking, and we'll bring you something to eat and drink."

Marie hesitated for a while, then nodded, and started to follow the female detective out the door of the room to a narrow hallway. She looked back at the male detective and he seemed to give her a slight wave goodbye. Marie didn't much care for him, as the way she saw it, he was the person who pushed her into this in the first place, so she didn't return the gesture.

Near the end of the hallway, they came to a smallish room, next to a bathroom. Detective Everhart led Marie into what was a bedroom with two plump chairs next to a small table and a large bed. Everhart motioned for Marie to sit down, and Marie chose to sit on the bed instead of a chair.

The detective gave her a puzzled look, and Marie shrugged and said, "It's more relaxing."

It was then that Marie noticed the tape recorder on the table, and apprehension filled her veins and she became motionless. The presence of the tape recorder made the situation very real, and there would be a record of what she told them, which the Swede would probably hear in court, and which would make him put a price out to every desperate thug in the area in return for her life. Because to a man like the Swede, it didn't matter that she was Vito Russo's daughter, he was so violent, so reckless, that he'd do anything to get revenge against those who betrayed him, including killing her.

"I don't think I can do this," Marie said, and quickly rose from the bed.

She ran to the door, but Detective Everhart stopped her.

"If you don't help us, we're going to have to arrest and charge you. You'll go to prison for a very long time."

"I won't," Marie snapped at her. "My father's got the best lawyers."

Everhart chuckled. "They're not going to be able to help you, not this time. We have more than enough evidence."

"I don't believe you!" Marie shouted at her.

"Suit yourself, but it's true. You're a pretty girl, you'll make someone a great girlfriend in prison."

"Fuck you," Marie replied, but inside, confusion drowned out everything around her. Marie *was* a spoiled brat, her daddy's girl, and she didn't know how she'd ever survive a brutal imprisonment. She glared at the detective, then slowly returned to the bed and sat down.

"Who the hell are you, anyway?" she asked Everhart.

"You know my name."

"I know, but how did you end up here with me?"

"You're my first assignment."

Marie laughed. "You just became a detective? That's all they think I'm worth, a fucking new girl?"

"No, I'm not a new detective. I'm just new to here. I was brought in from another city, to help with investigations."

"From where?" Marie asked, but before she'd finished, she knew the detective wouldn't answer her. "Forget it."

Everhart sat in one of the chairs and Marie turned away from her.

"I know you must be afraid," the detective said after a moment.

"Afraid?" Marie looked at her and sneered. "Do you not know who my father is?"

"Still, he can't always protect you."

"But you can, is that what you're trying to say?" Marie laughed.

Detective Everhart nodded.

"No one can fucking protect me from him," Marie said, her tears thick in her throat. "No one. Not even my father."

Everhart switched on the tape recorder.

"We know why you have the drugs, Marie. I don't think you're a dealer. We know about your gambling addiction."

"So? Maybe I need rehab," Marie replied.

Everhart shrugged.

The detective's indifference enraged Marie. "Do you have to use that fucking thing?" she snapped, pointing at the tape recorder.

"I do. Otherwise, we won't know what you said."

"So? Take notes. I don't want you using that fucking thing anywhere near me."

"I'm using it, Marie," Everhart replied, and her answer seemed final.

Now that she had been put in her place by the other woman, Marie's ego resurfaced.

She crossed her arms. "I'm not saying anything until I see what you bring me to eat."

"Quit acting like a spoiled brat," Everhart said, her face turning red as she lost her patience.

Marie rose. "You can't talk to me that way."

"You're very frustrating, Marie. We're trying to help you, and you're—"

"I'm terrified, okay?" Marie sat down again. "I'm fucking terrified." She held her head in her hands. "I don't know what the hell I'm going do," she whispered. "How am I gonna get out of this fucking mess?"

"You're going to talk to me, that's what you're going to do, and we're going to ensure that no one harms you."

"He'll kill me," Marie said faintly, as her heart felt like it had been ripped from her chest.

"Who will?"

Once she told them the truth, Marie knew there would be no going back.

"Marie?" Detective Everhart urged her to continue.

"They call him 'the Swede'," Marie finally replied. "I don't know his real name. I do know I'm just one of several people who hold stuff for him so that he stays under your radar. He said something about my shop being not too far from the docks."

"What's his connection to the docks?"

Marie shrugged. "Don't know."

"Marie." Everhart didn't sound convinced.

"I don't know. Honestly."

"Does your father know? Is he a part of this?"

Marie shook her head. "I would never rat on him, but he isn't, so it doesn't matter."

"Tell me more, and if it's substantial, maybe we can offer you a deal."

"Maybe? 'Maybe' ain't good enough."

"I don't make those kinds of decisions."

"Then call whoever does and make them give me a deal."

"You want me to call them right now, in front of you?"

"Yeah, that's what you're gonna have to do if you want me to talk to you."

"How do I know that you have anything good to tell me?"

"Oh, believe me, it'll be worth your while."

Detective Everhart stared at Marie quietly, then she said, "If I do this, you're going to need to work for us."

"Work for you? As what, a rat?"

The detective nodded. "You're going to have to wear recording equipment and go undercover."

"A rat! My father would fucking kill me if he finds out."

"But you said it has nothing to do with him."

"It doesn't. But he has strong principles."

"So do we."

Marie snickered. "Call them," she said, and she

couldn't decipher the other woman's expression, but the detective went to the phone and turned her back to Marie as she spoke into it.

Marie tried to overhear the conversation—

Russo's daughter.

Cocaine.

This could be big.

Detective Everhart ended the call and looked at Marie.

"You got what you wanted," she said.

"I want to talk to them," Marie insisted, moving towards the phone.

"You're really going to make me call them again?" the detective chastised her.

Marie just stared at her, wondering who would win this little game.

"I give you my word," Everhart spoke first, and Marie knew she had the advantage.

"Since when has a cop ever lied, right?" Marie said, with a rough chuckle.

The detective's face looked like stone, and Marie could see that she wouldn't relent. Marie couldn't have her father's lawyer confirm the deal because she didn't trust him. So Marie figured her best shot would be to proceed.

She told the detective what she knew about the Swede, and then hoped they'd put her on a plane to some place warm where she could hide out.

"So, where are you gonna take me? It better be some place nice."

"Not so fast," Detective Everhart said. "The Swede used your shop to stash his goods, but you said he had other hiding places. Where are they?"

"Don't know."

"Remember when I told you that you'd have to work for us? We're going to put recording equipment on you so you can find out."

Marie froze in panic. "You want me to fucking talk to him? Are you crazy? He's gonna kill me!"

"No, he won't be able to. We'll keep an eye on you," the detective tried to calm her down.

"You don't know him, he's a fucking maniac! He'll kill me, and it's not gonna be quick when he does it. You never said I had to talk to *him*."

"You'll have to do it."

"If I don't, then you're not gonna give me a deal?"

The detective nodded.

"You fucking tricked me, you bitch!"

"I told you that you'd have to go undercover. You should have assumed you'd have to see him, Marie."

"He's not gonna just tell me where he's keeping the stuff," Marie snapped at her. "If I ask him about it, he'll be suspicious."

"I'll coach you, and you'll be fine. Remember, if you don't help us, then there's no deal, and you'll go to prison."

"Fuck, that doesn't give me a choice, now does it?" Marie said, with a sigh.

CHAPTER EIGHTEEN

———◆———

TOMMY WAS AWAKENED by a knock on his door in the middle of the night.

"Who is it?" he demanded through the door, as he clenched his gun.

"Phoebe," a soft voice replied.

He tucked his gun into his waistband, so as to not frighten her, and opened the door.

"Hi," she said, beaming at him.

She looked beautiful standing there, the faint light accentuating her lovely figure, and for a moment, he didn't know what to say.

Phoebe seemed to sense he was hiding something. "Do you have a gun?" she asked, reaching behind him and touching his waist.

"You don't have to hide it, you know. I'm not afraid of them," she said, trying to grab it, but he wouldn't let her.

"Be careful, it's loaded, you'll hurt yourself," he told her.

"I can handle it," she said, giving him a grin.

One of his neighbors shouted at him to be quiet. Tommy took Phoebe's hand in his and led her into his apartment then closed the door.

"It's late. Why do you keep showing up here, at my place?" he asked her, not that he minded her being there.

"Why, am I tempting you too much?"

Tommy smiled.

"You can't keep coming here like this," he scolded.

"You'd rather I went to your pub?"

"Honestly, that might be better," he said.

"You're worried you might be tempted to take my innocence?" she said with a laugh, but her cheekbones flushed pink.

Tommy chuckled.

Phoebe walked with him into the living room, and he gestured for her to sit down.

"Your grandmother doesn't seem to like me very much," she said, making herself comfortable on his couch.

"She takes her time getting to know people," Tommy replied, settling down in a chair across from her, not wanting to tell her the truth.

"Why are you sitting all the way over there?" she asked him. "Do I scare you?" she said with a wide smile.

Tommy shook his head. "I scare myself," he said, looking at her.

Phoebe seemed to comprehend what he meant, but didn't appear fazed.

"I'm here to thank you for the favor you've done for me," she told him, rising and sitting in his lap.

Tommy gently pushed her off him. "Phoebe, what are you doing?"

"I'm trying to thank you," she said, turning away, unable to face him.

He heard her crying and knew he had offended her. Tommy rose and touched her shoulder.

"If we're going to go through with this, it has to be because you want to," he told her, and as he stared into her eyes, he saw that both of them knew what he meant.

"I do," she said, looking at him.

"Really? You're not just saying that because you feel like you have to 'reward' me? I don't want pity or a favor."

Phoebe glanced at his hand on her shoulder and placed her hand over his. Her warm, soft touch sent shocks of pleasure through him.

"I like you," she said, quietly. "That's my reason. But, somehow, I don't think you're the kind of man who needs to like a woman in order to sleep with her."

Tommy chuckled lightly. "You'd be surprised," he told her, with a grin.

Phoebe turned away from him and he assumed she was pouting, and it occurred to him how inexperienced she was.

"You've never done something like this before, have you?" he asked, grabbing her shoulder gently.

Phoebe glanced at him, her face flushed red. She shook her head a little and then looked the other way again.

"You can drop the whole 'sexy' act, I don't really like it," Tommy said, trying to make her feel better, but she turned to him and frowned.

"You don't like me?" She moved out from under his touch.

Tommy traced his fingers up and down her arm. "I didn't say that, Phoebe. Of course I like you, you're gorgeous and fun, but—"

"But you don't mix business with pleasure?"

"Exactly," Tommy said. "You're young, you have your entire life ahead of you. Believe me, you don't want someone like me to be your first."

"Someone like you?"

"Yeah, I'm not a good man, Phoebe."

"You know who my family is. I don't care what type of man you are. I like you, that's all that matters." She reached for his wrist and pulled her body close to his. "Be patient with me, that's all I ask. My last crush…" Phoebe whispered, then paused.

Tommy sensed something was amiss, and his voice deepened with concern.

"What did he do to you?" he asked her, tenderly brushing a lock of hair out of her beautiful eyes.

Phoebe looked away from him, and he touched her chin so that she was forced to meet his gaze. "Tell me."

"Nothing, it's not important."

The longer she wouldn't look at him, the more his suspicions grew, and he feared the worst.

"Phoebe," he ordered her to tell him.

"He tried to force himself on me, and when I wouldn't, he hit me. Okay?" She burst into tears and he held her.

"Do your parents know?"

Phoebe buried her face in his chest, and he could feel her shaking her head. "You're the only one I've ever told," she said, staring up at him, her pretty eyes shining with tears.

Rage filled his veins. "I'll fucking kill the bastard," Tommy told her, holding her body tightly against his.

CHAPTER NINETEEN

TOMMY HAD HEARD from Johnny that his men had been keeping an eye on the Swede's headquarters from a distance, and the Swede seemed to have abandoned his headquarters after they found Dana. Tommy arranged a meeting with Johnny at the pub early in the morning before they opened for the day, to discuss their next move.

Catherine had made them fresh coffee, and then went upstairs to make a phone call to their beverage supplier. Tommy watched the time tick by on the clock as he waited for Johnny's arrival.

A few minutes late, Johnny appeared in the pub's window and waved for Tommy to let him inside. Tommy rose from the bar to open the door. He typically kept the door locked during afterhours, as he never knew what sort of bad bastard might show up to cause trouble.

He greeted Johnny with a firm handshake and an open grin, not mentioning how he'd slept with Phoebe, of course.

"This is gonna be a short conversation," Johnny told him, looking around the pub and confirming they were alone. "But, obviously, it isn't wise to talk about things like this on the phone. You never know who could be listening in."

Tommy nodded in agreement and tried to decipher from Johnny's expression whether he had somehow discovered Tommy's night with Phoebe.

Johnny casually helped himself to a cup of coffee and Tommy still couldn't figure out whether Johnny knew. And if he did, how would he react? Very badly. Instantly, Tommy regretted being unarmed. Then Johnny set his cup down on the bar and sat. He gestured for Tommy to sit next to him.

Tommy stared at him for a moment and considered Johnny's intentions.

"I ain't gonna bite," Johnny said, as he drank his coffee.

Tommy almost replied, *I ain't fucking afraid of you*, but contemplated the wrath of a father whose daughter's innocence had been sullied by him, and stopped short of saying it.

"Death," Johnny suddenly said, looking away. "Death is what I've come to discuss."

Tommy laughed a little, but his insides churned. "Whose death?" he asked, trying to make light of the situation, although his body went cold as he felt all the color draining from his face. He tried to discreetly feel his pockets for a knife he sometimes carried.

"The Swede's, of course," Johnny said, looking at Tommy again, and Tommy stilled and could breathe once more.

It wasn't entirely that he feared Johnny's anger, which he did, but it was more the fact that Tommy cared for Phoebe and knew she'd never forgive him if he killed her father to save himself.

"You're gonna have to take this one, Tommy. It's your turn," Johnny said. "I got Anton, and now you gotta get this guy."

Tommy didn't hesitate to agree. He wanted to stay on Johnny's good side. "Sure, Johnny, I'll do it. It's only fair," he said with a chuckle.

It was not so long ago that he had been a policeman and upheld the law, and he even had longed to become a detective, and now he agreed to commit crimes without so much as a second thought. So much had changed, and everything had happened so fast that he had little time to feel guilty.

"The question is," he said to Johnny, "where the fuck has this guy gone to? No one knows where the hell he is."

"Wouldn't it be nice if he was already dead?" Johnny remarked.

Tommy smiled and shook his head. "Ah, but then I wouldn't get the pleasure of killing him myself."

Johnny let out a chuckle. "But, seriously, how are you gonna find him?" he asked.

"You mean, you're not gonna help me?" Tommy said, in jest.

"I could, but I don't think you need my help," Johnny replied with a smile and a shrug.

Tommy laughed, but it struck him then that while they were partners in a sense, they weren't brothers in crime.

"Don't worry about it," Tommy said. "I know someone who I can ask."

"Who?" Johnny said, his eyes darting this way and that.

"Why, are you suspicious of me?" Tommy asked him because he felt that Johnny was. "If we're gonna work together, you'll have to trust me."

"I don't know you very well."

"I know you iced Anton and I haven't said nothing to no one. Ain't that enough to trust me?"

"I suppose it should be," Johnny mused aloud.

"But it isn't?"

"I don't know, Tommy, but ever since I walked in here I've been getting the feeling that you're hiding something from me." Johnny pushed his coffee aside and faced Tommy.

Tommy started to laugh, then stopped when he saw the stony look on Johnny's face.

"Are you fucking serious?" Tommy replied, not knowing whether to be alarmed or offended.

Johnny's expression remained frozen as he nodded.

"Don't be fucking paranoid," Tommy responded quickly, desperate to control the situation. "You know who I'm gonna ask? I'm gonna ask Dana. All right? I'm not hiding a fucking thing from you."

The truth was that Tommy did have something to hide from Johnny, however— the fact that he'd slept with the man's daughter, but he couldn't tell him that, of course.

Johnny rose from the bar to look him in the eye. "You're sure that's all there is to it?" he asked, and Tommy could barely control the urge to throttle him.

The only thing that kept Tommy from brutalizing Johnny right there on the spot was the thought of Phoebe's sorrow and hatred towards him if he carried it through.

"Yeah, that's all there is," he answered, keeping his gaze on Johnny's, unwilling to allow the other man to dominate him.

Johnny nodded and went to the door to leave. Suddenly, he stopped in his tracks and turned to Tommy. "You're gonna see her?"

"Who?" Tommy said, not a little unpanicked, unsure whether he meant Phoebe.

"Your old girl, Dana."

"Oh, right. I'll go see her."

"What if she won't tell you anything?"

"She will," Tommy insisted.

"Fucking confident, aren't you?" Johnny said with a chuckle on his way out. "Thanks for the coffee."

Tommy went upstairs to tell Catherine he was leaving for a while, and she knew better than to ask him where he was going. He wanted to approach Dana at home rather than via the phone, as he felt that in person, he could convince her to give him the information he sought. He knew that Dana had avoided going into her office ever since her kidnapping and was hiding out at her apartment. So far Tommy had managed to persuade her not to go to the police about her ordeal, although he didn't know how long that would last now that he'd told her he no longer had feelings for her.

"Tommy, it's early, what are you doing here?" she spoke through the door when he knocked. Surprisingly, she didn't sound happy to see him.

"I need to see you," he answered.

"Now isn't a good time," she replied, and he knew she wasn't alone.

At first, Tommy thought she had spent the night with some guy, then he became concerned she was being held against her will by the Swede or his men.

He pounded on the door. "Dana, what's going on? Let me inside!"

The people in the neighboring apartments yelled at him to be quiet.

Dana opened the door in her bathrobe, her face flushed from annoyance.

"What the hell, Tommy?" she shouted at him.

Tommy made his way past her into the apartment, but her bedroom door was shut.

"Who's in there?" he demanded to Dana.

"I don't know, some guy I meant at the pub last night. I can't remember his name, but he doesn't know that. He was good-looking and fun, so I took him home. Am I allowed? What do you care, anyway? You don't own me."

She was right, of course. He shouldn't have cared. But he did. Although he no longer loved Dana, he couldn't bear the idea of her being with another man, no matter how little the guy meant to her.

Tommy made his way to the bedroom door to kick it open if he had to, but Dana stopped him, standing between him and door.

"You don't get to do that, Tommy. I'm not yours anymore."

The smug look on her face made him want to slap her, but as a personal rule, he didn't harm women.

Tommy stepped back a little and watched her aggressively. "This isn't like you, Dana. Taking a stranger home for the night like a whore."

"Fuck you!" Dana spat at him.

"Everything okay out there?" the other man shouted from behind the closed door, apparently unwilling to come out and see for himself.

"What a fucking pussy this guy is," Tommy muttered as he cleaned Dana's spit from his shirt.

"Why, because he isn't acting like a thug like you?" Dana shot back. "You don't even know him."

"You don't either," Tommy said, with a smirk. He paused. "I can't believe you fucking spat at me," he said with a laugh.

Dana looked at him and started laughing as well.

"We're fine," she told the man in her bedroom through the door. "Stay there. Don't worry." Then she looked at Tommy.

"What are you doing here?" she asked him. "You know how I feel about you, and you've already told me you don't feel the same way, so why do you care if I spend the night with someone else?"

"I didn't come here to spy on you," Tommy said after a moment. "I burst in because I didn't know what was going on. I thought something might be happening to you. It's not so surprising after what you've been through."

"You came here to check on me?" Dana said, a smile of pleasure forming on her lips.

"Yeah, that's it exactly," he said because it was what she wanted to hear. He couldn't tell her outright that he'd gone there because he wanted something from her. He had to flatter her a bit first.

"Well, as you can see, I'm doing fine," Dana told him, but she blushed a little, and he knew she liked that he was concerned about her. Then she frowned.

"You can drop the act, Tommy. I can tell you came here because you need something from me."

"I can't fool you," Tommy smiled.

"You sure can't. I'm not one of your silly girls."

"Hey, there's no one else," he replied, then he thought of Phoebe, who wasn't a silly girl.

"You're lying," Dana said, and he shrugged. "But it's fine. What do you want?" she asked him.

Tommy gestured at the door. "Not with him here. I'll tell him to leave," he said, trying to walk past her into the room again.

"You'll do no such thing," she said, shoving him back gently. "You can tell me what you want right here."

He made her move to a more private area, away from her bedroom door.

"You're not going to like this, but I need to find out where the Swede is. He's abandoned his usual place."

"Why would I know where he is?" Dana questioned.

"You were watching him for Johnny. I thought maybe he might have mentioned something."

"I don't know what to tell you, Tommy. Why do you want this information? I'm assuming your intentions aren't good."

Like him, Dana had once been a cop. Now, also like him, she was an ex-cop. But Dana didn't come from a family like Tommy's. Her father, too, had been a policeman. Although she had to despise the Swede for what he'd done to her, Tommy doubted she would easily divulge his whereabouts if she had any idea of where he was or any suspicion of what Tommy might be intending to do. But over his time with Dana, he'd learned that she didn't tolerate bullshit and it was best to be honest with her.

"What do you care, after what he did to you?"

"Tommy, I hate that bastard with all my heart, but you know my values."

"And you know mine. Think of this as your revenge. You just have to tell me what you know. I won't tell you what I'm gonna do. That way, if it comes up, which it won't, you can say you don't know anything."

"Tommy, you know what you're asking me to do, don't you?"

He looked at her and nodded, and she shook her head.

"Think of what he did to you," Tommy urged. "He would have killed you, after his two thugs had their fun torturing, assaulting and then raping you. You know it."

Dana didn't budge. So he kept going. "Have you forgotten what they did to you? Starting with kidnapping you in broad daylight? You don't think the Swede knows where you live? You think he can't get to you? How well do you know that guy in your bedroom now?"

Dana put her hand to her face as if in shock. That didn't seem to have been something she'd taken the time to consider, despite her years of training in law enforcement. She looked over at her bedroom door and sighed. Maybe, Tommy thought, she was considering whether the risk she'd taken with that guy had been worth it.

"You've worn me down," she said, with a tone of defeat. Then she looked up at Tommy. "When I was watching him for the Garcias, I once heard him briefly mention another location."

"Where is it?" Tommy asked, unable to control the excitement in his voice and his lust for blood.

"Let me think." Dana turned away and walked over to the window, biting her thumbnail as she was trying to remember. She looked out the window and then quickly pulled down the shade.

"Is something wrong?" Tommy asked and quickly went over to the window.

"No," Dana answered. "I just thought it would be better to keep the shade down. For privacy."

"Yeah, for privacy," Tommy retorted, not convincingly, as he glanced over at the bedroom door.

Dana either didn't hear him or pretended not to. Suddenly she snapped her fingers. "I know! Something like, dive...or dive-all...or..."

Tommy took her by surprise when he ran up to her and grabbed her by both shoulders and kissed her on the cheek. "I know what area you're talking about—Devil! Zuiden Duyvil! It's the area by the bridge not far from where we used to work. I think there are some old tunnels near there from years ago that are no longer used for anything. That could be where he is."

Dana seemed subdued. "Be careful, Tommy," she spoke with genuine concern. "He might not be alone. He could have other thugs with him just as bad as the ones who . . ."

She didn't have to say more. Tommy knew what she meant. Now it was time to get going and do something about it. He started to make his way to leave. "That fucker better treat you well," he said, gesturing over at the bedroom as he opened the door to the apartment.

"Or what?" Dana said with a knowing smile.

"You know what," Tommy gave her a wink.

"Tommy, promise me you won't destroy yourself," she whispered to him on his way out.

He looked back and smiled sadly. "You know I can't promise that."

Dana sighed, then wondered aloud to herself, "Zuiden Duyvil? What does that mean, anyway?"

"South Devil. It's south of Spuyten Duyvil, which is Dutch for 'in spite of the devil'."

Tommy smiled to himself as he closed the door to Dana's apartment. He had a job to do. He went home to get his gun, a long knife, and some rope and construction tape. After the horrors the Swede had put his mother and Dana through, that fucker was going to pay big time, and his death would be slow.

———

As the sun began to vanish for the day through the room's curtains, Marie called the Swede on his burner phone from the safehouse where she was staying.

"It's Marie," she spoke when she heard him answer.

"Marie. I haven't heard from you in a long fucking time. I know what happened to your beauty shop. Where's my stuff? No one better have found it, or else you're a dead bitch."

"You can't talk to me that way! You know who my father is!" Marie shouted, and Detective Everhart, standing at her side in the room, calmed her.

"What the hell did you just say to me?"

"Nothing, forget it," Marie mumbled.

"You better hope I forget about it." He paused. "You calling to tell me where my stuff is?"

"Yeah," Marie tried to her best to sound convincing. "I managed to move it all before the firemen arrived."

"I've been trying to find you," he told her, and she wondered whether he doubted her story. "If you really have my stuff, where is it?"

"I don't want to say over the phone," she carefully replied.

"Is someone there with you?" he asked in an

agitated whisper.

"No, no one's with me, but you never know who might be listening in. I have everything of yours. Everything is safe."

"It better be safe. I pay you good money, you ungrateful bitch."

"I said it was safe."

"Yeah? Where the fuck is it, then?"

"I said I can't say over the phone. Let's meet so I can tell you."

Marie waited in silence for his answer, with Detective Everhart staring at her, anticipating her reaction.

"I'll pick you up from your apartment and we can talk in my car," he finally said.

"No," Marie said, then paused when she real-ized how loud she sounded. She feared being trapped in such an enclosed space with him, from where she couldn't flee. "How about the alley behind *Mickey's Pub*," she suggested. "You know where that is?"

"Yeah."

Marie knew the pub would be crowded and it wouldn't be easy for him to harm her with all those people coming and going.

"You'll go there in an hour," he told her, want-ing to control the situation.

Marie mumbled "Okay" and then ended the call.

"Are you meeting him?" Detective Everhart asked her eagerly.

Marie nodded.

"Alone?" Everhart asked.

Marie shrugged with the phone still clutched in her hand. "Doesn't matter," she told the detective. "He always brings his thugs with him."

"When are you meeting him?"

"In an hour."

Detective Everhart nodded. "I'll go tell my boss."

When she returned with the equipment for Marie to wear, she gestured for Marie to undress.

Marie pointed at the door. "Close the door first."

"Why are you so shy all the sudden?" Detective Everhart remarked.

"I gotta have some dignity."

The detective sighed, then went to shut the door.

But Marie *was* a bit shy, as her mother had instilled in her the virtues of being a good Catholic girl, and so she asked the detective to look away as she disrobed.

"I'm going to have to look at you when I put this on you," the detective said, holding out the equipment, which didn't look too terribly uncomfortable.

"I know, but just while I take them off."

Marie quickly undressed and then cleared her throat. "I'm ready," she said, and Everhart looked at her once more.

The gear felt cold and harsh against Marie's bare skin when the detective put it on her.

"Is he going to be able to tell I'm wearing this?" Marie asked.

"He won't notice a thing," Everhart assured her.

"You're sure? Because if he does, I'm a fucking dead woman."

"Trust me, I do this all the time."

"My family don't trust cops as a rule."

"I'm sorry, Marie, but you're just going to have to trust me on this. Put your clothes back on."

Marie slowly dressed, and they went downstairs, where Everhart and her boss quickly ordered Marie outside into an unmarked dark van.

Marie was silent on the drive to the meeting, and Detective Everhart, seeming to sense her apprehension, avoided speaking to her. They stopped a good distance from the pub and promised they'd be watching her and listening in, then Everhart gave her a nod of encouragement and Marie jumped outside.

Marie stood still for a moment in the quiet street and breathed in deeply. The day had turned dark, and her hands shook as she went towards the alleyway alone, the undercover gear seeming to weigh her down, although it was light-weight enough. She could smell her own pungent sweat and tried not to gag. Marie feared the Swede more than she feared anyone. More than she feared her own father.

As she neared the pub, she could hear the pulsating beat of music and see the glare of lights. More people began to walk around her, towards the pub, their conversation and laughter causing her head to throb. Marie cursed at them to be quiet in a whisper, then mumbled, "Not you," because she assumed the detectives were listening.

She peered through the darkness at the alley as she approached but didn't see anyone there.

"He's not here," she said, though she knew they wouldn't respond.

Marie willed herself not to panic. Maybe he was just late, but as long as she'd known the Swede, she'd always known the man to be on time, if not early. Had something happened? Did he suspect she had gone to the police?

Fear chilled Marie's veins as she stood in the empty alley. What if the Swede did arrive after all, only to come to kill her?

Marie knew that if she bolted right then, there would be no going back. She told herself to give him a few more moments.

A man stumbled out of the pub side door and leaned against the brick wall, vomiting. He stood up and leered at Marie and began to amble towards her.

"Get away from me!" Marie shouted as she retreated to the street.

He fell down onto his hands and knees and chuckled as another man exited the pub and helped him to his feet. The man sang an old pop song as the other man walked him out of the alleyway, past Marie.

Marie went back into the alley. Her legs began to give out and she felt as though she might faint. She put her hand to her head as she waited, struggling to balance herself.

A woman screamed in the distance and Marie jumped and looked around. The scream was followed by raucous laughter from the same woman.

How much time had gone by? The pub hummed then roared with activity and she reasoned the place must have been at its peak capacity for the evening.

Marie sensed it was time for her to leave. The Swede wouldn't be coming. And what did that mean? What would the police do if she couldn't give them what they wanted? Would they abandon her to his wrath?

———◆———

In Tommy's mind, the fucker didn't stand a chance. He'd put the rope and tape in a bag and slung it over his shoulder as he made his way to the bridge near the tunnels, dark and desolate even for the Zuiden Duyvil area.

Tommy knew he might be walking to his death, that the Swede's men might ambush him, but at that point, he didn't care. The Swede had ordered his mother's murder and his thugs had violated Dana, and because of those things, Tommy would risk anything, even death, to even the score. The one night he'd spent with Phoebe had been enough for him to die a satisfied man.

His feet crunched on discarded glass as he went past the bridge, with the swooshing sound of traffic overhead, the moving cars causing the bridge's metal base to clang and vibrate and hum all at the same time. Tommy found himself alone, save for a homeless man passed out in front of one of the bridge's large columns. Tommy almost shouted at him to check that he was alive, then stopped because any noise would draw the Swede's attention to him.

Would the Swede be there, hiding out like the little bitch that he was? Or was Dana wrong and he'd already abandoned that place, too?

Tommy slowed his pace as he went closer and saw the glare of a light shining ahead. He stopped and listened.

He heard a faint sound then felt a sharp blow to his head and collapsed onto the hard, filthy ground.

"Fuck," he said, touching the spot at the back of his head where he had been struck. His hand felt damp with blood. Then he saw a man standing above him, not the Swede, but one of his thugs, a wide, giant of a man.

Shit. He needed an equalizer. Fast.

Tommy reached into his waistband and pulled out his revolver, firing up at the hulking shadow. The man's face exploded in the air and his flesh and blood sprayed Tommy. The man dropped to the ground next to Tommy and he saw a gun being held limply in the man's hand. Tommy hadn't known the other man had been armed, and he'd taken a chance by reacting first. But he knew what men like them would do to him if they took him alive: they'd torture him to death, and take their time with it.

With the sound of the gunshot likely having reached the Swede in the tunnels, the light in the distance went out and someone, the Swede probably, shouted, "What the fuck was that?" Tommy had to move quickly. He jumped up with the bag still slung over his shoulder.

His plan had been ruined, and he wouldn't be able to sneak up on the Swede and capture him alive. He wouldn't be able to tie him up and make him suffer for a while. He'd have to out-right attack him and get it over with quickly to make sure it happened at all. He figured a knife would be his best chance at inflicting the most damage in the most fast but painful manner.

In the darkness, Tommy struggled to approach the tunnels from the back where the Swede wouldn't be expecting him. He tripped on a bot-tle and it went rolling against the ground. Tommy winced, then continued treading fast, but more carefully.

Near the other end of the tunnels, he stopped and watched in silence, his faint breathing the only sound he heard.

Tommy went up to the first tunnel slowly and he could see the outline of a man shorter than him. The Swede? Before he gave the other man a chance to pull a weapon on him, Tommy charged at the man's back with the knife raised in his fist and quietly plunged it into the guy's neck. And again, and again. He did it for his mother and for Dana. Blood gushed out of the man, splashing against Tommy, feeling warm, then cold on his skin. He continued to go at him, like a feral wild animal. The man cried out and landed on the ground, squirming around Tommy's feet.

Absolutely enraged, Tommy considered sinking his teeth into the man, but didn't want to leave a mark the police could use against him. He turned the body over with his foot, saw the blond hair, and knew he was the man known as the Swede.

"Rot in hell, you bastard," he said.

CHAPTER TWENTY

D ANA SAT AT her kitchen table, having coffee and a cigarette for breakfast. She rarely
smoked, only when she had a lot on her mind,
and that morning she did. She had watched the
local news earlier and there was a report on a man
being brutally murdered inside the tunnels near
where she and Tommy had once worked together.
And another man had been found shot to death
outside. Dana had called a detective friend of hers
and casually inquired about the deaths, and it was
he who had confirmed what she'd thought, that
a man fitting the Swede's description had been
killed in the tunnels. She knew who had com-
mitted the crime, of course. Tommy. And, in a
way, she'd helped him.

Dana sat there, debating whether she should
call her detective friend back and give Tommy
up. Tommy had saved her life, but turning him in
would be the moral thing to do, and Dana had
always had strong morals. Even Tommy knew that.
But knowing and loving Tommy had changed
her, weakened her, and Dana had become what
she never wanted to, a woman who would do

anything for a man who no longer desired her. With Tommy, loyalty came first, and Dana knew that if she handed him over to the police, he'd never forgive her, and there wasn't anything she couldn't bear more than his hatred.

After the murder Tommy went home to shower and change, rang Johnny with the news, and then went to bed.

With the Swede's death, Tommy saw a way to success. Starting that very morning, he used the information Dana had given him to take over the Swede's operation with the barges, and he brought in Johnny to help him. Soon, because of his newfound wealth, Tommy had even purchased a nightclub that he planned to renovate and transform into something even bigger, a start to fulfilling his dreams of boundless success. He could have easily betrayed Johnny and not given him a piece of the action, but something told him that it was better to have Phoebe's father on his good side.

Sure, Dana might tell what she knew someday, but Tommy didn't believe she would.

Marie spent her first night in jail miserable, quietly crying on the uncomfortable bed in her dark, damp cell, with her lunatic cellmate talking to herself in the bed above hers.

With the Swede dead, she'd lost her bargaining chip with the police, and they'd locked her away.

Her own father felt she had betrayed him and wouldn't post her bail.

All she could think about when she wasn't crying, was that little bitch Phoebe, the reason she'd ended up in there. How could she get revenge? And how would she escape this place to do so?

Marie knew she wasn't going to be released any time soon, given the charges she faced, but there was one person she could still depend on to help her. The only person in the world who loved her no matter what she did. Who, unlike her father, could overlook her shortcomings.

Her mother, Isabella.

Marie had been allowed one phone call to the outside on her first day in prison, and she rang her mother at her hotel. Isabella kept asking her how this could have happened and why wasn't Vito helping? Clearly, she didn't know the details. But Isabella pledged to help in any way she could, including sending a Marie a lawyer since Vito had refused.

Isabella would do anything for Marie, and Marie knew this. Marie also knew her mother still had the gun that Vito had given her when they were together to protect herself from any harm that might come from being associated with him.

Marie couldn't discuss the issue directly with her mother on the phone, that would be too risky, but she had to somehow send a message to her.

The next morning Marie was woken by a guard, at an hour so early that only some sparse light trickled in through the bars of the cell's sole small window.

Half asleep, Marie struggled to rise from the bed.

"Get up," he ordered.

"What the hell is going on?" she mumbled, only partly comprehending the situation.

"Your lawyer is here to see you," he answered.

An idea passed through Marie's mind and she shot up and stared at the tall, burly guard, a large man whose dark blue uniform barely contained his big stomach.

She would figure out a way to send the message to her mother through the lawyer.

Marie got out of bed and the guard opened the cell door, gesturing for Marie to follow him. She hoped her mother chose a good lawyer. Since she wasn't considered a violent offender, the guard didn't put handcuffs on her.

She hadn't eaten breakfast yet. Although the food inside the prison was terrible, the coffee wasn't too bad and she wanted some before her meeting.

"Can we stop for a coffee?" she asked the guard.

He chuckled and shook his head. "What does this look like, Starbucks?"

Marie shrugged at him then rolled her eyes when he wasn't looking.

The guard suddenly stopped in his tracks, forcing Marie to stop as well.

"You want coffee?" he said. "Maybe if you give me a blowjob, you can have some before your visit," he said with a laugh.

"You're joking?" she said, because she couldn't tell.

He stared at her and shook his head.

"Look," Marie told him. "No offense, but I'm not doing that just for a cup of coffee."

"I had to try," he said, and whistled to himself as he resumed walking.

She shook her head in disgust and continued following him outside the area with the cells to the visiting room. She peered over his shoulder and saw a bespectacled man in a disheveled suit sitting at one of the tables. In fact, he was the sole person in the room. Her lawyer. He had messy hair and seemed young and inexperienced, and Marie wondered what the hell her mother was thinking. Isabella wasn't wealthy, so perhaps he was the best she could find. Someone young and inexperienced could be to Marie's advantage given what she had planned.

The guard moved away from in front of Marie and told her to sit at the table. The lawyer quickly rose to shake her hand.

"Am I your first ever client?" she asked him, with a wink.

The young man blushed and let go of her hand. He mumbled, "You're my first paying client, yes," then quickly sat down and removed a folder from his briefcase.

Marie sat across from him and smiled.

"And your name is?"

He seemed very flustered, then replied, "Sorry, it's Bradley Jones."

"My mother hired you," she said.

"Yes, she did."

"Did she tell you about why I'm in here?"

"A little, yes, and I have your file here." He waved it around and some papers flew out onto the floor.

Marie shook her head as he leaned down to retrieve them. He was utterly hopeless, but he was hers. "Do I scare you?" she asked with a smile.

He quickly shook his head, but his face reddened.

"Look," she said. "I don't have anything new to share with you. They're keeping me in here because my mother doesn't have enough money for bail and my father won't help. So, there isn't much for you to do. But I need you to do a favor for me."

Bradley adjusted his eyeglass and stared at her. "What do you need me to do?"

Marie glanced over her shoulder at the guard who stood in the corner watching them.

"Do you have a pen and some paper?" she whispered.

He arched his eyebrow then searched through his briefcase and handed her what she wanted.

"I suppose you wouldn't have an envelope…?" Bradley fumbled in his briefcase some more and retrieved a somewhat worn-looking envelope.

"That'll do. I need you to take a message to my mother for me. You can't let anyone read it. Even you can't read it. Is that clear?"

"I'm not sure if I'm supposed to—"

Marie cut him off. "Do you want to get paid?" she asked.

"Yes, of course."

"If you don't help me, then I'll tell my mother not to pay you, and she and I are very close, so she'll do anything for me. Do you understand?"

Bradley frowned, hesitated for a moment and seemed to be thinking, then nodded.

Marie began to write on the piece of paper, leaving much said in what she left unsaid:

Ma—

You know what happened with Phoebe. That bitch is the reason I'm in here.

Keep an eye on her for me. You know what to do.

Love,

Marie

Marie folded the paper, quickly put it in the envelope, checked that the guard wasn't watching, and gave it to the lawyer.

"Guard this with your life," she told him. "You know who my father is. I am my father's daughter, and I am capable of doing anything if you don't do as I say. Understand?"

He looked at her apprehensively and then put the note inside his briefcase.

Marie rose and gestured at the guard, "Guard, we're done here."

She rang her mother again during the prison's allotted phone call time later in the week.

"Ma?" Marie said. "How is everything?"

"Not bad, considering. How are you?"

"Not bad. I met Bradley Jones."

"What did you think of him?"

Marie laughed slightly. "What do you think?"

"He stopped by to see me the other day," her

mother said.

"And?"

"Count me in, my Marie. I'll make sure everything's perfect."

Another woman stood behind Marie waiting for her turn and Marie could feel her eyes on her.

"Thanks, Ma," Marie spoke into the phone, grinning from ear to ear. She ended the call and started to walk away back to her cell.

"What the fuck are you so happy about?" the woman behind her asked Marie as she left.

"I have my reasons," Marie replied with another smile, and the woman laughed.

———

A few weeks later, Tommy awoke to the phone ringing at his bedside.

"Who is it?" he said, his mind cloudy from sleep.

"It's me," Phoebe's voice replied.

There weren't many people he'd let bother him so early, but she was certainly one of them.

"My parents know about us," she blurted out.

"What?" Tommy sat up, immediately awakened by her words. He rubbed his forehead in shock. "How do they know?"

"I told them this morning at breakfast. I love you, and I don't want us to have to hide."

She sounded so young, and Tommy shook his head. He liked the girl, but what the hell was he getting himself into?

"Phoebe, you shouldn't have done that," he scolded.

"Well, I'm sorry, but I did. You have to come to my parents' house now to talk to my father. He's really upset."

"Shit," Tommy muttered.

"What's wrong?" Phoebe sounded hurt.

"You shouldn't have told them, Phoebe. Look, I like you, but it was a stupid fucking thing for you to do."

"But I love you," she insisted. Phoebe didn't seem to mind that he'd never spoken the same words to her.

"Do they know what I did to Marie Russo for you?" Tommy asked.

"No." Phoebe sighed. "Tommy, are you gonna come or what?"

Tommy knew that he would break her heart if he refused to go, and Johnny would break his neck, so he agreed to visit. He had to make things right somehow.

He dressed and went outside to his car. The traffic was light, and he arrived earlier than he anticipated.

Camille stood on the manicured lawn in her bathrobe, silhouetted against the soft morning light, waiting for him, waving her cane in the air like a weapon and yelling curses at his car.

"Oh, shit," Tommy whispered to himself. He had his gun on him, but hoped not to use it.

Tommy parked nearby and exited the car with his hands in the air, trying to appease her. He looked around for Johnny, concerned he might get attacked from behind, and then Phoebe came running out of the house, trailed by her father, whose gold neck chain beat against his chest.

"You've ruined my little girl, you bastard!"

Tommy felt like chuckling at the entire scene. What exactly had Phoebe told her parents? Tommy panicked and got down on his knees in front of Phoebe.

"You got it wrong," he told Johnny. "I'm in love with this girl."

Johnny was practically holding a gun to his head, so Tommy continued, looking at Phoebe, he said, "Let's get married."

Phoebe beamed at him and nodded, then she embraced her parents.

Fuck. What the hell had he just done? But not doing it would have been the loss of his business partnership, and maybe his life.

Phoebe wanted to get married by next week, but Tommy managed to convince her to wait a few months. He imagined she would have married him tomorrow if she had her way!

There was still one very important person he needed to deliver the news to.

Tommy returned to the city and went to the pub. By the time he arrived, his grandmother had already opened the place for the day, so Tommy took her into a private room they rarely used to tell her about his impending marriage.

Catherine shook her head at the revelation and sat down on some boxes to collect herself. "Tommy, do you love this girl?" she asked, looking at him. "You hardly know her!"

"She's not bad," he replied. "Marrying her is good for business, and she's a nice girl."

Catherine reached out and touched his hand. "Sit down," she told him.

Tommy tilted his head. "What's wrong?" he asked.

"Sit."

He sat next to her and she continued touching his hand, her skin feeling warm and worn against his.

"I have to tell you something important," she said.

Tommy looked at her and shrugged. "What?"

"It's about your mother," she said matter-of-factly, almost dully. After a moment, she continued. "Violet is alive," she whispered, turning her head away from him.

Tommy let go of her hand and jumped to his feet.

"What the fuck are you saying?" he demanded.

"She's alive and safe."

"Why are you doing this to me?" Tommy shouted as he paced around the room, the space feeling smaller than it was.

Catherine kicked the door closed with her foot. "I told you she was dead because I thought she might not recover and because I wanted her to be safe from whoever did this to her. And, I wanted you to get on with your life and run the business. Tommy, she was in a coma for months and months."

"You bitch, you fucking lied to me!" Tommy went towards her and Catherine ducked out of his reach as if she thought he would strike her.

Catherine went on. "After the ambulance

picked her up here, I went with them and made some calls to a man I've known for a very long time. He's affiliated with a private rehabilitation clinic in Switzerland, and he didn't hesitate to pay any expense to have her flown there to be cared for and made whole again. It's a top-notch place, Tommy. The best."

Tommy stilled and breathed heavily. He wasn't happy with his grandmother's dishonesty, but gradually he reasoned she had had no choice. Then reality set in. His mother was alive!

"I don't like that you lied to me." Tommy paused. "Ma's gonna be so fucking angry with me for getting involved with Pheobe," he said with a chuckle, sitting down next to his grandmother.

Catherine gave him a knowing smile. "She sure is."

Tommy shifted and a book fell out from under the box where he sat. He reached down to pick it up. It looked like a journal.

"What the hell is this?" he asked his grandmother.

She took it from him. "I've been wondering where this was. It belonged to my father, your great-grandfather."

"I always wanted to know more about him," Tommy said.

"It's time to bring your mother home," his grandmother said after a moment, standing up. She waved the journal around. "It's going to be a long trip, so we'll bring this with us. We'll have lots of time to talk about everything you want to know about my father."

CHAPTER TWENTY ONE

THE FIRST PERSON Tommy wanted to share the news about his mother with was Phoebe. Before that, it would have been Dana, but Tommy didn't want to run to her any longer.

He rushed to the women's clothing shop in the city where Phoebe would be at work by then. He hoped to catch her on her lunch break.

Tommy arrived at the shop and found one of Phoebe's co-workers, a charming older blonde woman, folding sweaters near the entrance. She looked over at Tommy when he entered and smiled.

"How can I help you? Are you looking for something special for the lady in your life, per-haps?"

"Actually, I'm here to see Phoebe. I'm Tommy. I'm not sure if she's mentioned me."

"You're Tommy! Of course Phoebe has men-tioned you, but you're even better looking than she said."

Tommy chuckled at her flattery.

The woman introduced herself as "Barbara". Then said, "Phoebe told me you two are getting married. Congratulations!"

Tommy thanked her, and for a moment he wondered if she'd embrace him, then when she didn't he asked, "Is Phoebe around?"

"Yes. She's in the back. I'll go bring her out." Barbara put down a sweater she had been about to fold and opened a door behind them. "Just one moment," she said with a smile, then disappeared inside the other room.

A few moments later, Barbara emerged with a beaming Phoebe, who looked as fresh and pretty as ever.

"Tommy!" she said and ran into his arms.

Sometimes Tommy wondered if Phoebe was so crazy about him because he had been her first, but she was a gorgeous, sweet girl, and marrying her would be good for his family's business.

Tommy held onto Phoebe tightly while Barbara watched them with a wistful smile.

"What's going on?" Phoebe pulled away and asked him, with her brow furrowed in concern, as though he might have come to call off their engagement.

"It's nothing to worry about," he assured her, stroking her face. "Can you give us a moment?" he asked Barbara, who smiled sheepishly, then stepped away to help a customer who just entered.

"Tommy, what is going on? You have me worried," Phoebe told him.

"There's some news I have to tell you."

"Tell me, Tommy!" Phoebe demanded, unable to control her concern. Her face reddened as she watched him.

"Don't be upset," he told her, lightly touching her arm. "It's nothing to do with you."

"What is it, then?" She tapped her foot impatiently.

Tommy led her by the arm to a private corner. "I don't know how to say this, so I'm just going to go ahead and tell you. My grandmother just told me that my mother is alive."

Phoebe stepped back and stared at him in shock. "What? You told me she died. That's what my parents also thought."

"I know. That's what I believed, too. But it turns out, my grandmother lied to me."

"Why the fuck would she do that?"

Phoebe rarely cursed, and so her reaction surprised Tommy.

"She wasn't sure if my mother would recover," Tommy answered. "She wanted me to move on with my life."

"I'm sorry, Tommy, but your grandmother's a bitch to do something like that to you. It's really fucked up."

"She isn't like most grandmothers," Tommy said in defense.

"Where is your mother, then, if she's alive? How is she gonna feel about our wedding? I know you mentioned she doesn't like my parents."

"But she'll love you," Tommy replied, and grabbed her and kissed her to assure her.

"You're sure?" Phoebe asked him, rather naively, as she gazed up at him.

"I'm very sure," Tommy said, although he knew how much his mother disliked Phoebe's family. He pondered how he would tell his mother about his relationship with Phoebe.

"Where is your mother, anyway? You never said. Is she still in New York?" Phoebe asked him.

"No, she's far away."

"Where?"

Tommy sensed she wouldn't stop asking until she gave him an answer, so he said, "She's in Switzerland."

"What the hell is she doing there?"

"She's at a hospital; she's been in a coma."

"A coma? Does she remember you?"

Tommy had been too wrapped up in excitement when his grandmother told him the news to consider that and he hadn't asked her.

"I'm not sure. I hope so," he answered after a few moments.

"Of course she'll remember you!" Phoebe said cheerfully, with kindness in her eyes.

"You're a real sweetheart," he told her, and gave her a wink.

"What are you going to do next?" Phoebe asked him as another customer entered.

"I'm going to bring her home."

"I'll go with you. Let's go," Phoebe said, and started to leave to tell Barbara, who was struggling to manage both customers at once.

"No," Tommy said, holding her back gently. "You stay here and help Barbara. We won't be gone for that many days."

"Days?"

"It's far away," Tommy reminded her.

"You said '*we* won't be gone'. Who are you

going with?"

Tommy smiled to himself because Phoebe acted as though he planned to bring another lover along with him.

"My grandmother is coming with me," he said after a moment of enjoying her jealously.

"Oh," Phoebe replied, seeming slightly embarrassed but relieved. After a moment she said, "You know, Tommy, there's something I want to talk with you about. I was actually planning to talk to you tonight, but then you showed up here, so I guess I'll just say it now."

"What is it?" Tommy asked, becoming concerned.

Phoebe sighed. "My Dad told me that you used to be a cop. I didn't know that about you. Why did you hide that from me? I feel like I don't know everything about you."

"You'll never know everything." And that was how he wanted to keep it. Tommy wanted to remind her they'd only known each other for a few months, but answered bluntly, "It's not something I tell most people."

Phoebe looked away in frustration then turned to him again. "But, Tommy, we're getting married! Don't you think you should've told me that?"

"I probably should have, yeah. I don't know why I didn't. I guess I thought it didn't matter."

But Phoebe came from a crime family, and so *did* it matter?

Phoebe put her arms around his waist and looked up at him. "You know I still love you, right? Even know you used to be one of them."

Tommy felt relieved but he wouldn't show it. "Them?" he asked instead.

"You know, cops."

Up until then Tommy hadn't considered that she wouldn't want him if she knew the truth about his past, but given her family's history, he wasn't very surprised by what she said.

"I should leave now," he told her, and kissed her goodbye. He gave her a gentle push in Barbara's direction.

As Tommy left he felt Phoebe's eyes on him, watching him walk away, but he didn't turn back to look at her.

CHAPTER TWENTY TWO

WITH THE NEW money Tommy made from taking over the Swede's drug business, he was able to arrange for a private jet to take his grandmother and himself to Switzerland to bring his mother home to the apartment he'd recently bought for his grandmother, knowing that Catherine would want to remain near her recuperating daughter at all times.

They weren't planning to stay in Switzerland very long, just one night, and so Tommy only brought along a small suitcase, but when he went to the pub to pick up his grandmother in a taxi, he found she had a large bag with her. He asked the driver to park and went outside to help her.

"Why are you bringing all this with you?" he said.

"Take it easy. I brought some of your mother's things. She'll want to look nice on her journey home. I would assume they mostly have her wearing sweatsuits there."

"All right," Tommy said, because there wasn't any point in arguing with her when it came to matters of Violet's happiness. "Did you lock up the pub?"

Catherine nodded. "You know, Tommy, I had a thought," she mentioned as the taxi driver exited to put her bag inside the cab.

"And what's your thought?" Tommy asked as he waited for her to enter and sit down.

"We should sell the pub," she told him as he hunkered down to enter and sat next to her.

Tommy nearly froze. The pub had been in his family for generations. "Mother won't like that idea," he said. "She loves the pub with all her heart." And although he'd never admit it aloud, Tommy sort of loved it as well.

"Yeah, but once she's home, she might not be up to managing it, and I'm getting older," Catherine said as Tommy closed the door.

The driver got in and they started on their way to the airport.

"There's me," Tommy said to his grandmother. "I'll manage it."

"No, Tommy, you're too busy. You have the business, which is our family's legacy, and I'm so proud of you. And you're getting married. I'm sure you'll be having children soon—"

"The pub is also my family's legacy," Tommy interrupted her. "I wouldn't mention any of this to my mother, by the way. You'll only upset her if you do."

Catherine patted his hand. "Don't worry, I won't. She's gonna be so happy you're finally getting married."

"I don't know about that," Tommy said with a chuckle. "She doesn't exactly have a great history with Phoebe's family." Then a very unpleasant thought occurred to him. "She doesn't still think they had something to do with her injury, does she?" he asked.

"No, she knows who was responsible."

"You told her?"

Catherine nodded.

"Still doesn't mean she likes them," Tommy muttered sarcastically.

"Give her time," Catherine suggested. "Don't be afraid to tell her."

"I'm not afraid," Tommy insisted.

Catherine let out a dry laugh. "Tommy, you don't have to lie. This is your mother we're talking about." She paused then said, "Can I offer you a little advice?"

Tommy agreed to hear it because he knew she would give it to him no matter what he answered.

"If there's one thing your mother loves in this world as much as us, it's the family business. Push that angle to her. Marrying Phoebe Garcia will be good for the business."

"Yeah, but I'm marrying her enemy's daughter, for fuck's sake. Is she really ever gonna accept that?"

"Listen, Tommy," his grandmother snapped, suddenly seeming irritated. "You chose to screw the girl and then she ran to her father afterward, so you'll just have to think of something to tell your mother."

Her anger surprised him, but he didn't react.

They rode the remainder of the trip to the airport in silence, with Catherine opening her window and quietly smoking a cigarette and Tommy unable to concentrate on the passing scenery.

At the airport, the taxi driver let them off at the private section and unloaded their bags. Tommy paid him and tipped him well. An attendant greeted them and took their luggage away. Another escorted them inside the private lounge where there were a few business people and a waiter brought them complimentary martinis after they sat down.

Catherine removed a book from her jacket pocket and Tommy saw that it was his great-grandfather's journal that he had found earlier. "We can talk about this on the plane ride there if you'd like," she casually mentioned as she sipped her drink and Tommy knew it was her way of apologizing to him for her outburst in the taxi.

"All right," he said, then looked at the large clock on the wall. "We'll be leaving soon," he told her as he rose.

Catherine tucked the journal back inside her pocket.

Tommy left a good tip for the waiter, then led his grandmother to the boarding area for private jets.

"Are we really going to be the only ones on this plane?" she asked him.

Tommy nodded. "Yes, and it's a jet, not a plane," he said with a smile. "And you better get used to traveling this way, because it's only the best for us from now on."

"My father would be so proud of you," Catherine said, with sadness in her eyes, and tears catching in her throat. "We'll have no need to worry from now on."

Tommy gave her another smile, but deep inside, from experience and his family's history he knew how wrong life could go—and how fast that could happen.

"Don't worry," Catherine told him, seeming to sense his thoughts. "Nothing's going to happen."

But Tommy wasn't as sure.

A beautiful young flight attendant with full lips and large breasts, her dark hair arranged elegantly under her blue cap, greeted them in a soft, warm voice, and escorted them inside the private jet that had a dazzling interior with white leather seats and sunlight pouring through the glistening windows. Tommy noticed a television and bar in the corner. Everything about their surroundings, from the flight attendant to the inside of the jet, was absolutely perfect.

"Oh, my, Tommy," Catherine said, taking in all the elegance at once and patting the edge of her dress as though its simplicity concerned her.

"You look stunning," he reassured her. "You fit in perfectly. This is all ours for the time being, so let's enjoy it."

"Easy for you to say, you're wearing a suit," she replied in jest.

The gorgeous flight attendant showed them to their seats and her red-lipped smile revealed beautiful teeth.

Tommy thanked her and his grandmother nudged him when she caught him staring at the young woman's backside.

"Phoebe wouldn't like that very much, now, would she?" Catherine said.

Tommy shrugged, but in his heart he still didn't know if he could be loyal to one woman forever.

Catherine gestured to their surroundings. "Are we taking your mother home in this?"

"Yeah," Tommy said. "She'll be more comfortable." He paused. "Is she fragile?" he said, because he'd wondered that before but never had asked his grandmother the question. He'd been too worried about the answer.

"She's a lot better than she was."

"I feel terrible I wasn't there for her. When she woke up, did she think I'd abandoned her?"

Catherine shook her head and patted his hand. "No, she never thought that. I told her about my plan."

"She was okay with it?" Tommy asked, a bit hurt that they both had deceived him.

"She knew I was only looking out for you. She knew it was best. Why, are you angry?"

"Don't worry about it," Tommy replied, concealing the truth, not wishing to argue again.

The attendant sauntered over and offered them each a flute of bubbling champagne.

"I could get used to this." Catherine grinned as she touched her glass to Tommy's.

Tommy nodded, "Me too."

Catherine set down her champagne on the tray by her elbow and her brow furrowed. "You're sure you aren't spending too much money, Tommy?"

"Hell, no," Tommy said with a laugh. "There's

so much coming in."

"Even though you're sharing it with them?"

Them. Phoebe and her family.

"Yeah, sure. Relax, everything is gonna be fine. It's gonna be great." Tommy patted her arm.

"I just hope you inherited my father's sense for business," Catherine remarked.

"I'm sure I have," Tommy said defensively, and although the money came in quickly, he, too, sometimes fretted how quickly it was leaving. At least Phoebe's parents were paying for the wedding.

The attendant asked them to put on their seatbelts as the jet took off. Once they were in the air, they removed them and Catherine took the old journal out of her pocket and set it down between their seats.

"We have a long trip ahead," she said to Tommy, then it felt like she was watching him. "You know, Tommy, you remind me so much of my father. I think you'll do very well for yourself, actually, and for us," she added with a smile. "Do you know how my father got his start in this crazy business? Did your mother ever tell you?"

"No, she never said much about him."

"It's painful for her. She loved him greatly, and when he died, she was lost for a long time."

"They were close?" Tommy asked, because his mother had spoken little about the matter.

"Yes, very. You want to know more about your great-grandfather? Let me tell you a story."

Tommy signaled to the flight attendant to refill their glasses, and once she had, he sat back and listened, with the sky outside a faint blur of blue.

"My father Sean, he was Irish, which you already know. And his mother was Scottish. Your generation has it easy, but when my father was growing up a lot of the Irish had a hard time in America because many people resented them coming here. My father saw how his own father, an Irish immigrant, struggled, and he didn't want that for himself. So he managed to get an education, but he still had a hard time finding work that paid well enough to suit his ambitions. At one point, he considered changing his last name, but knew his father wouldn't speak to him again if he did. So, what did he do instead? Lots of the young guys in the neighborhood where he grew up become gangsters, so that's what he did. And he found he had a knack for it. He started way down and worked his way to the top. He married my mother along the way, a pretty and shy French girl. She was a class above him socially, but, my God, there were never two people more in love than them."

Tommy found the tale intriguing, but with the calming motion of the plane riding in the sky, he closed his eyes to the sound of his grandmother's soothing voice.

CHAPTER TWENTY THREE

———◆———

A WHILE LATER, SOMEONE nudged him awake, and as Tommy opened his eyes with a grin, he expected to see the gorgeous flight attendant by him.

His grandmother frowned. "Did you really think that's who I was?" she said with a laugh, reading his mind.

Tommy shrugged. "A man is allowed to dream." He looked out the window as white-capped mountains came into view below an endless clear blue sky.

It was the next morning in Geneva.

"We're here," Catherine said.

Someone, the flight attendant, probably, had cleared away their champagne glasses. A sleek black luxury car waited for them when they landed, and Tommy quietly slipped the flight attendant a hundred-dollar bill and a wink out of his grandmother's view as they deboarded with a chill in the air. He knew his grandmother wouldn't approve of him throwing money around, but the girl just was too beautiful for him to resist.

Tommy had arranged for them to stay overnight at a hotel near the private rehabilitation hospital where his mother was staying. The hotel was far from the airport, and the drive there gave Tommy a chance to see the city and its grand architecture, a mix of old and new, surrounded by those soaring, white-dotted mountains in the distance, as he imagined he wouldn't be spending much time there once they collected his mother. He had business to attend to in New York and a wedding to prepare for.

He had been a little unsettled ever since Catherine had mentioned the idea of him having children with Phoebe. Tommy hadn't thought of that going into his proposal to her. Was he ready to be a father? Did he even want to be one? His own father hadn't been present very much in his life growing up, and so Tommy hadn't really learned how to be a father himself, and his mother's boyfriends certainly couldn't count as role models. Part of him longed for children of his own to love and pass on his legacy, and Phoebe certainly had good looks to pass on to them, but the other half of him didn't wish to bring children into a world that he knew could be very cruel to those vulnerable to its clutches. With Tommy's success, came an increase in the chance that a rival would wish to harm him, perhaps through his family, and he couldn't trust that harm would never come to his children. Phoebe knew this firsthand, as the daughter of gangsters, and from the traumatic ordeal she'd experienced herself.

Tommy decided then, during the car ride to the hotel, that he wouldn't bring up the matter with Phoebe. He would let fate decide instead.

The car dropped them off at the hotel, a large place steeped in old-fashioned elegance, where an attendant collected their luggage after ushering them into an elevator with gleaming gold buttons, and showed them to their very comfortable rooms on one of the high levels.

Tommy wanted to change out of his suit and rest for a while, but Catherine insisted they visit Violet at the hospital straightaway.

"Are you nervous?" Catherine asked him when they were alone in the elevator on the ride down to the hotel lobby.

"No, she's only my mother," Tommy said with a shrug, though his stomach churned slightly in anticipation of the visit.

"Yes, she's your mother, that's why you should be nervous," Catherine said with a soft laugh.

In the lobby the hotel manager rang a taxi for them, which arrived quickly. Tommy got in after his grandmother.

"Do you speak English?" he asked the driver, an older man wearing a wool cap.

The man nodded and smiled at him.

"You'll accept American money?" Tommy asked him. He hadn't had time to exchange the bills at the airport. Tommy offered him more money than the trip would likely cost, in the hope that it would make a difference.

"Yes, thank you," the man said and eagerly took the money from him.

"You gave him too much," Catherine murmured to Tommy.

"No, this way there won't be any issues," Tommy insisted.

"Suit yourself, it's your money to spend. But remember what I told you about being careful. It's a lot easier to lose everything than you might imagine."

Tommy nodded at her because she wouldn't stop going on until he did, but he was young enough he wasn't too worried about the future.

The private rehabilitation hospital looked tall and imposing in the distance, with a neat line of leafy trees surrounding it. Even the outside of the white building radiated order and cleanliness. It reminded Tommy that he needed to think of something fast to tell his mother about Phoebe.

"The guy who helped pay for all of this," Tommy spoke to Catherine, "I'd like to pay him back."

Tommy disliked accepting charity from anyone.

His grandmother waved away the idea. "That's not needed," she told him.

"But I have money now," he replied.

"No," Catherine spoke firmly. "He helped her as a favor to me, because he wanted to."

"What is he, an old lover of yours or something?" Tommy asked, half joking.

The look on his grandmother's face didn't suggest he was wrong.

"She's my mother. I don't like him paying for her, whoever he is," Tommy said in a resolute tone. "I will pay him back today."

"With what? A handful of cash? It's not like you have a checkbook or can just go to an ATM or walk into a bank. People like us, we can't keep money in banks."

She was right, of course, as she always was. Tommy had brought cash with him, but not enough to cover his mother's hospital bills.

"Besides, I can't offer to repay him," his grandmother continued. "If I do, he'll think we're rude. He has enough money to take care of it, believe me."

The taxi stopped near the hospital and Tommy and his grandmother exited. The day had warmed and the sun shone on them with full force as they entered the building. Tommy wished he'd had the chance to change into something more comfortable.

Inside the hospital lobby, a young woman greeted them in a cheerful manner in English, seeming to sense they were foreigners once they entered, and with a laugh to himself, Tommy wondered how it was so obvious.

Tommy started to explain to the girl who they were there to visit, but Catherine interjected.

"Please tell Dr. Frank Matthews we've arrived," she told the girl, and since Tommy's grandmother was a woman who earned your respect as soon as you looked at her, the girl nodded and ran off to use the phone behind the large desk in the lobby to page the doctor. There were few other visitors about given the early hour, and Tommy and his grandmother were the only ones waiting to be allowed upstairs.

A few moments later, a tall and handsome older man, with a distinguished headful of white hair, exited the elevator and approached them. His eyes glowed with admiration upon seeing Catherine. He wore a white coat and looked like a doctor.

Tommy had many questions to ask him. Had his mother's mind been damaged somehow? Would she remember him? Initially, he assumed she would recognize him, but standing there in the lobby, he wasn't as confident.

Dr. Matthews spoke in an American accent, and Tommy wondered how the man knew Catherine and how he'd ended up living in Switzerland.

He shook Tommy's hand and embraced Catherine for longer than Tommy thought was polite.

Suddenly, he felt protective of her. "How do you know my grandmother, if you don't mind my asking?" Tommy spoke to Dr. Matthews who had just stepped away from Catherine.

Catherine shot him an annoyed look. "Tommy," she started to say.

But Tommy wanted to look out for his grandmother, so he asked Dr. Matthews, again, "How do you know her?"

The doctor gave him a look that told Tommy he recognized him for what he was: a thug trying to make trouble for him.

"Your grandmother and I met a long time ago. I was a friend of your grandfather's," he answered Tommy with grace.

Tommy didn't know much about his late grandfather, who had died young under strange, tragic circumstances, as his grandmother didn't speak of him often. Tommy recalled he had been a small-time politician and that his grandmother had emphasized how gangsters and politics were often connected. Tommy had lost touch with that side of the family over the years.

Tommy acknowledged the doctor's answer with a nod, and Catherine quickly changed the subject.

"How's my daughter doing?" she asked Dr. Matthews.

"I was just visiting her," he replied. "She was awake when I left her and in high spirits."

"Will she remember me?" Tommy quickly asked.

"Of course she will," Catherine interrupted.

Dr. Matthews told Tommy, "Your mother had brain surgery, but she's doing very well considering."

"But will she remember me?" he asked the doctor.

"Tommy, she knows who you are," Catherine said, not unkindly. "She'll remember you."

"All right," Tommy said. "Let's go see her."

CHAPTER TWENTY FOUR

—◆—

TOMMY AND CATHERINE followed Dr. Matthews inside the elevator and after a quiet ride, arrived at the floor where Violet stayed.

"Can my mother walk?" Tommy asked the doctor. They hadn't brought a wheelchair along for her and he worried she might need one.

"Yes, she's walking well," he replied. "She has received the best therapy here."

"Thank you again for your help, Frank. We're very grateful," Catherine said with a warm smile. She waited for Tommy to also express thanks.

Tommy knew he should thank the doctor, but his stubbornness prevented that at the moment and he ignored his grandmother's stare.

The hallway, glistening white floors and walls, fanned out into a section of rooms, which seemed spacious from the outside. The door to one was ajar and Tommy could see his mother in bed. What sounded like Swiss news played on the television. From where he stood, Tommy couldn't tell if she was awake. Dr. Matthews encouraged Tommy and his grandmother to step into the room, then excused himself after being paged.

Tommy stood at the side of Violet's hospital bed, unsure of what to do. Catherine stood at the other side of the bed, looking at her grandson with a concerned gaze. The rehab hospital had taken good care of Violet, and her beautiful red hair fanned around her face, across her pillow. He could hardly see the area where she'd been wounded. Dr. Matthews was obviously very talented. Tommy thought she looked like a sleeping angel. Which was ironic considering who his mother was, as she certainly wasn't an angel in real life.

Both Tommy and Catherine were hesitant to wake her, but she opened her eyes when a nurse entered to check her vitals.

"You have visitors," the nurse spoke to Violet in a thick accent. She smiled at Tommy and Catherine then exited the room.

Dr. Matthews returned. "Violet, your family is here to see you. They came all this way to bring you home," he said, and she finally looked at Tommy and Catherine.

Tommy became worried he'd been lied to and that she didn't recognize him. But only for a few seconds. She gave him a huge smile, and her eyes seemed tired, but Tommy saw she knew him.

"I'll leave you to chat," Dr. Matthews said, and exited.

"Tommy, my boy. It's a beautiful day," Violet said to her son, peering out the window that overlooked the city and the mountains. The sunlight caused the different shades of red in her hair to sparkle.

Tommy was a tough, hard man, but he bent to his mother's level and embraced her and told her how much he loved her. She stroked his face lightly.

"I thought I'd lost you," he whispered, standing up and touching her hand. Her skin felt smooth and cool.

"I thought I'd lost myself," she replied.

"What was it like for you, while you were asleep all this time?" he asked.

"The funny thing is, I don't remember anything. I don't remember being shot. Do you know who shot me? On the phone your grandmother mentioned Camille and her husband had nothing to do with it, but she didn't say who was responsible."

"You have nothing to worry about, they've been dealt with," Tommy said, not wanting to involve his mother in the matter. He didn't want any trouble to come to her, all he wanted her to focus on was recovering. "I took care of it."

Violet struggled to sit up in bed and her frailty shocked him. "Tommy, tell me who it was," she said, unable to accept his answer.

Catherine approached the bedside. "He just said he took care of them. Don't upset yourself, Violet. There's nothing for you to worry about. Isn't that right, Tommy?" she said, looking at him.

"Yeah, you just keep getting better. Don't worry about nothing," he told his mother with a smile.

Violet seemed reluctant to accept their wishes, then she asked him for a glass of water.

Tommy searched the room and found a pitcher

and cup on a table by the window. He poured some water into the glass and handed it to her.

"I hope it isn't too warm," he said.

"Doesn't matter," Violet said as she sipped the water. When she finished, she gave the glass back to him and he set it down.

"Tommy," Violet said as Catherine fussed over her daughter's comfort, tidying up the magazines on the hospital tray and tucking a blanket around her.

Tommy smiled at his mother.

"I don't want you to be upset with your grandmother," she told him. "You understand why she had to lie to you, don't you?" she asked carefully.

"I think so, yeah. I don't like it, but I think I can understand."

"When she told me what she did, I didn't like it at first, either, but then I understood why she did it and knew it was for the best for everyone."

When Tommy didn't speak, Violet said, "I don't want there to be any trouble between you two."

"There isn't," he responded, acknowledging his grandmother with a nod. "We're fine."

"What have you been up to all this time, Tommy?" Violet asked after a moment. "Your grandmother mentioned you're doing very well for yourself, of course we didn't discuss specifics on the phone. So, what's been happening?"

His mother was back, all right, and was still her old self, excited and eager for news of the goings-on in the family crime business. But Tommy wanted her to have less control this time around, and he sought to remind her that the family business was now his.

"Don't you worry, Ma, I've got everything taken care of," he said with a smile but a firm undertone.

Violet's expression hardened, and Tommy knew how difficult it was for her to take a step back and let him run the business. Then Catherine gave her a look and said, "It's time to let the boy run the show, Violet, and he's already doing very well for himself and for us."

Violet finally nodded, then smiled at Tommy.

"Any new women in your life?" Violet casually asked him.

Typically, there had been several at a time. Now there was only the one.

Tommy knew right then he had to tell her about Phoebe. He was marrying the girl, so it wasn't like he could hide her from his mother forever. But being familiar with the history between the two families, made him hesitate.

"Tommy, what is it?" his mother asked, immediately sensing his reluctance. "You've met someone, haven't you? I hope you haven't started a relationship with that Dana bitch again." She started to scold him, then Tommy interrupted.

"No, not with her. She and I are done. But she isn't a bitch."

"She tried to get me thrown in prison. She's a bitch."

"But nothing happened, did it?"

"Only because you took care of it."

"She isn't the one I'm marrying," he said, then realized what he'd just said.

"Marrying?" Violet was able to sit up this time and stared at him with her mouth wide open. Tommy somewhat expected her to jump out of bed and demand answers from him. "Tommy, you're getting married? When the hell did this happen? Who is she?" Violet suddenly turned to Catherine. "Why the fuck didn't you tell me about this?" she demanded.

"Because of how you're acting right now," Catherine replied in a cool tone. "I wanted for Tommy to tell you himself."

"Why? What are you hiding? Who is she?" Violet asked her, and when she didn't answer, she stared at Tommy and said, "Who is the girl?"

Tommy knew he couldn't escape her wrath forever, so he looked at her and said resolutely, "Phoebe Garcia."

"Camille's fucking step-daughter?" Violet asked, very much her old self again.

Tommy nodded.

"How the hell did you two meet?" she demanded.

"Our families are working together now," Tommy said. "That's what I've arranged, and that's why we've been so successful."

"Are you fucking kidding me?" Violet said, starting to rise from the bed, but Catherine stopped her. "You did all this behind my back," she told Tommy. Then she looked directly at Catherine. "And you let him."

"It gave us the best chance," Tommy explained, "and we're doing so fucking well, Ma."

"Is she pregnant? Is that what happened?" Violet said. "Because if she is, you don't have to—"

"She's not," Tommy cut her off.

"Do you love her?" Tommy went quiet, and Violet said, "You don't seem sure."

"Listen, it doesn't matter. She's a sweet girl."

"I'm not sure if I can accept this," Violet said, turning away from him and looking out the window.

Catherine sat down in a chair near the hospital bed and Tommy looked around for a place to sit but found none.

"It'll be good for the business," Tommy said after his mother had cooled down. "I've been able to re-establish our place in the neighborhood and in the entire city."

Violet didn't respond, then looked at him and smiled. "I know it will be. I'm happy for you, and for us."

"You're not angry?" he asked in shock.

Violet shook her head. "No. In fact, before I was shot, I planned to make some kind of deal with Camille to get her off my back."

"I can't believe it. Are you kidding me?"

"No, it's the truth."

Tommy nearly laughed at the irony.

"Did you know about this?" he asked his grandmother.

"This is the first time I've heard about it," she replied.

"But I'll never be able to forgive Camille for what I know she did to Max," Violet added.

Max, Violet's mentor, the man who had murdered Camille's father many years ago, had vanished under mysterious circumstances years later, and was never seen or heard from again.

"But I guess I can accept her stepdaughter as your wife," she continued.

Tommy had the feeling his mother could learn to accept anything if it helped the family business.

Catherine smiled at both. "See, it all worked out in the end."

Then Violet said to Tommy, "I need to know who shot me."

Tommy sensed she wouldn't stop asking until he told her.

"The Swede was the one who did it, but he didn't do it for Camille and Johnny," he said. "He did it to cause trouble and start a war between our two families so then he could take over everything himself while we were distracted. He wanted to steal the whole fucking neighborhood. Anton helped him."

"Anton?" Violet said faintly, and Tommy knew the revelation, and her former lover's betrayal, stunned her. "No, it can't be true."

"I'm sorry, Ma, but it is. He's gone now, so you have nothing to worry about."

Knowing what Tommy meant by 'gone', Violet nodded and stared at her hands.

"I know how much you used to love him, and I was fond of him, too," Tommy said. "But he had to go. There wasn't another way." He stopped short of apologizing.

"All he did was bring you trouble anyway," Catherine commented from where she sat, and Tommy willed her to shut up. "You know I love you, sweetheart," she told her daughter. "But Anton really was a piece of shit. It really is for the best."

Violet's face turned scarlet, and her rage made the room seem small. Sensing she would explode at Catherine, Tommy moved out of the way. He braced himself for the argument.

"You hardly knew him," Violet said calmly instead, surprising both Tommy and his grandmother. "We don't have to talk about it anymore. I trust Tommy had a good reason. He wouldn't have let harm come to someone he was so fond of unless he absolutely had to."

"Let's go home," Catherine said, rising from the chair. "Tommy got us a nice place to live."

"You mean, I don't have to live above the pub anymore?" Violet asked with a smile.

"Only the best for you two from now on," Tommy told them.

Then something unpleasant seemed to occur to Violet. "You didn't sell the pub, did you?" she asked them.

"No, nothing like that," Tommy replied with a glance at Catherine, thinking about what she'd said.

"We're still running it," Tommy continued speaking to his mother. "And we hired a couple of trustworthy people to help out."

Dr. Matthews entered the room with the paperwork Violet needed to sign to leave the hospital tomorrow and Catherine thanked him again for his help with everything.

"My pleasure," he told her with sincerity, and

Tommy felt a little guilty he'd been so hard on the old bastard.

He quickly thanked him and shook his hand.

"I brought you some clothes," Catherine told Violet.

Violet thanked her. "How are we getting to New York?" she asked Tommy.

"A car service is picking us up from our hotel early tomorrow morning, then we're collecting you here, and going to the airport. We're flying home on a private jet," he said with a grin, knowing she'd be pleased.

"A private jet? You're joking."

"No, I'm not."

His mother erupted with ecstatic laughter. "Tommy, you've done so well for yourself, for us. I'm so proud of you," she said, reaching to embrace him, and her words meant more to him than he believed anything ever would.

CHAPTER TWENTY FIVE

THE LONG JOURNEY home to New York had taken a heavy toll on Violet, and Tommy set her up in the apartment he'd bought for his grandmother, which she would now share with his mother.

Tommy and Phoebe spoke on the phone and she told him how eager she was to meet his mother, but Tommy didn't think Violet was quite ready for that just yet. He bought Phoebe a large diamond ring and she was already showing it off to her friends.

"I hope your mother likes me," she said, during a phone call later that week.

"She will," Tommy replied to comfort her.

"Can you come to dinner at my parents' house tonight?" Phoebe asked him.

"Why? What's going on?" he asked carefully, not wanting to insult her, but also not really wanting to eat dinner with her parents.

"Why?" Phoebe spoke in frustration. "Why not? We're getting married, Tommy. You're gonna have to do things like this."

Tommy didn't like anyone telling him what to

do, not even sweet, sexy Phoebe. "Don't speak to me that way ever again," he told her firmly, revealing a darker side she likely didn't know he had. But she'd have to get used to it if she was going to be his wife.

"Tommy, please," Phoebe complained, changing her tone to a softer one, and trying to win him over that way. "I have some news to share."

He'd underestimated her and didn't believe she would find being married to him challenging.

"What news?" he asked her, sounding concerned. What had happened while he was abroad? Did she want to cancel the wedding? He would find that somewhat of a relief, but his mother seemed excited by the idea of strengthening their business through the marriage and he didn't know how she'd react to bad news.

"It's nothing awful," Phoebe replied. "You'll find out when you come to dinner. Please come."

"Fine," Tommy said, and was about to hang up, when Phoebe gave him the time to arrive at her parents' house and then asked if she could say hello to his mother.

"Not now," Tommy told her. "She's still weak. You'll meet her soon."

"I understand," Phoebe said, but she sounded disappointed.

"I'll see you later," Tommy replied.

Early that evening, Tommy left his mother to rest under his grandmother's watchful eye and went outside to buy a bottle of fine wine to take to Phoebe's parents' house as a gift. A short while later, he walked to the garage near his apartment where he kept his fancy, new blue sports car. He planned to buy a boat soon that he and Phoebe could enjoy using on the weekends at the river. But he still lived in the same small apartment. Phoebe wanted them to move into a house near her parents' after their marriage, but they were living in separate places for now, as Phoebe's father was very traditional, and they had already looked at a few homes in the area. Tommy didn't love the suburbs, but he knew that's what married couples did, and he also figured that Phoebe expected them to have a big family someday.

Tommy drove his car to Phoebe's parents' house and parked near their driveway, like he always did when visiting the home. He exited with the nice bottle of wine in his hand, wondering what news Phoebe had to share but reasoning perhaps she just wanted to see him.

Phoebe must have seen him coming down the walkway, as she opened the door before he reached the front steps.

She ran outside to embrace him, not paying attention to the wine he held. But she was still young and didn't appreciate the finer things in life yet.

The porch light illuminated her fine beauty. "I missed you so much!" Phoebe practically shouted and wouldn't stop kissing him.

Tommy enjoyed her affection, for a moment, but after she kept at it, he became exasperated and gently moved her off him and indicated that they should go inside. He had to remind himself of her age and that she didn't know any better than to smother him with her warmth.

"Dinner is ready," Phoebe told Tommy as she welcomed him inside the house and closed the door. Then she called out to her parents, "Tommy's here!"

Camille and Johnny entered the room and greeted him. Camille's sparkling top highlighted her light eyes, and Johnny wore an expensive designer business shirt and suit jacket without a tie.

He shook Tommy's hand, rather strongly, Tommy thought, and then Tommy went to embrace Camille, but she tensed so he never followed through. He shook her hand instead and handed her the bottle of wine. Camille thanked him and showed appreciation for his taste.

"Tommy, welcome," Johnny said.

Ever since Tommy had asked Phoebe to marry him, the air filled with tension whenever he and Johnny were in the same room. Johnny never said it outright, but the feeling he radiated to Tommy implied, "You better not break my daughter's heart."

Tommy didn't know if the vibe was intentional, or merely because Johnny was Phoebe's father and it was his instinct to protect her, but it made Tommy a little nervous. He knew that when it came to Phoebe, there would be no going back and if he did anything to upset her, what he'd worked so hard to build would implode.

"How was your trip?" Johnny asked him. "Phoebe told us everything. I must admit we were shocked to hear the news about your mother, but

I guess it all worked out for the best in the end, right?" he said with a grin.

Tommy managed a smile in return, somewhat relieved they weren't angry about Violet's condition being concealed from them and the consequences of that happening.

"That's true," Tommy replied. "I didn't even know myself."

"I can't believe your grandmother would hide something like that from you," Camille blurted out. "I don't mean to offend you or her, but in my opinion, that's very fucked up. I'd never do that to my grandson, if I had one."

Phoebe shot her a look and Camille backed off. Tommy's loyalty to his grandmother prevented him from agreeing with her, so instead of reacting he pulled Phoebe close to him and said to Camille with a smile, "Maybe you will have a grandson someday."

"Let's eat before the food gets cold," Johnny quickly said, ushering them into the dining room. "Camille made steak."

Camille had set the table elegantly, with tall crystal glasses and silverware that gleamed from polishing. Before his success, Tommy would have felt out of place in such a home, and even now he struggled not to stare too openly at the glittering crystal-and-gold chandelier above the large dark-wood dining table. When they sat down to start with Tommy's wine, Johnny pulled out one of the stylish chairs for Camille at his side and waited for Tommy to do the same for Phoebe. She smiled up at him and thanked him.

Tommy sat down next to her and somewhat expected a maid to serve them, but after drinks were started, Camile rose and entered the kitchen then returned with the steak served on expensive plates. She gave Tommy his first, then Johnny, and, lastly, Phoebe and herself.

It was only when Camille sat down again and they began to eat that Tommy noticed Phoebe hadn't touched her wine. Mid-bite, Camille also fixed her gaze on her step-daughter and said, as if contemplating aloud, "You like wine, but you're not drinking. Pheobe, what's wrong? Are you ill?"

"I'm not ill," Phoebe spoke quietly.

Camille stared at her in silence. "You aren't pregnant, are you?" she said with a nervous laugh.

Phoebe didn't respond.

"You are, aren't you?" Camille said. She dropped her fork and the sound startled Tommy.

He looked across at Johnny, who seemed shocked at the reminder that Tommy had slept with his daughter before marriage, and Tommy started to chuckle at the man's reaction then ceased. He wondered if this was all some sort of practical joke Phoebe was playing on them, but his insides churned.

Johnny had stopped eating entirely by then. He stared at Tommy like he could murder him right there on the spot. Then he said coolly to his daughter, "Is this true, Phoebe?"

She looked down at the table and nodded. Tommy stared at her in absolute shock, but she wouldn't acknowledge him.

"The wedding will happen *very* soon," Johnny

stated to everyone in the room. "I am not walking my daughter down the aisle if she's showing and having everyone think you two are only getting married because you screwed her." He rose, pointed his finger at Tommy, and raised his voice. "I will not fucking be ashamed at my daughter's wedding!"

Camille looked at Tommy. "Did you know about this?" she demanded.

"It's news to me," Tommy said casually.

"You bastard," Johnny shouted at him, his face reddening.

"Please, can everyone stop fighting?" Phoebe suddenly yelled, tears coming through her voice.

Tommy figured he ought to put his arm around Phoebe and support her but, still shocked by the news, he didn't react.

Phoebe sniffed back tears and mumbled that her father was being, "Old fashioned" and "Over-reacting as usual", then she turned to Tommy and said, "But my dad's right. We need to get married really soon, or else we'll bring shame to my family."

Tommy watched her and didn't respond. Then he wanted to run away screaming. It was all happening too fast. The engagement. Now a pregnancy, and being forced to get married even faster. Although Phoebe charmed him, he'd only agreed to marry her in the first place because he needed to stay on the good side of her family. And a part of him had taken comfort in the fact that he could always try to leave her in a year or two if the marriage didn't work out, but a baby changed everything. With a child in the picture, Tommy would be bound to Phoebe forever.

Tommy didn't flee. Instead, he turned to Phoebe, and calmly said, "You're sure you're having a baby? You never said anything to me about this."

Phoebe laughed a little and seemed younger than she was. "Tommy, I think a girl knows when she's pregnant."

He considered asking her for proof, then Camille rose and stood behind Phoebe and placed her hands on her step-daughter's shoulders protectively. A look of affection passed between the two women, and Tommy recalled Phoebe telling him how she'd recently learned that Camille couldn't have children of her own and how that had affected her parents' relationship. Tommy imagined that a grandchild would mean a great deal to Phoebe's step-mother.

Camille gazed at Tommy. "If my daughter says she is, then she's telling the truth."

Johnny sat down and didn't take his eyes off Tommy. "The wedding will happen immediately," he said in a tone that conveyed the finality of the situation. His eyes dared Tommy to disagree.

Tommy weighed his options, with Camille glaring at him and Johnny giving him a murderous stare. Phoebe was beautiful and charming, and he could easily see himself falling in love with her, but he wasn't yet. What choice did he have at the moment? If he walked away from the marriage with Phoebe at that moment, it would also mean walking away from the business partnership with Phoebe's family. Doing so would anger them greatly, and who knew what they might do?

Tommy didn't fear anyone, but he knew the many advantages of a good business relationship and his ambitions went far beyond his neighborhood, and far beyond his city, and he needed Phoebe's family's cooperation to accomplish these goals.

He decided to accept the news. For now.

Tommy looked over at Phoebe and smiled. "A baby? That's really great news. We'll get married whenever you'd like, as soon as you'd like."

"Really?" Phoebe asked him, and he could feel Johnny's and Camille's eyes on him.

"Of course," Tommy replied, maintaining his smile.

Phoebe sat there quietly and blushed. Johnny nodded at him, and Camille sat down and they resumed having their dinner.

CHAPTER TWENTY SIX

A FEW DAYS LATER, Violet felt better enough for Tommy to take both her and Phoebe to lunch at an upscale restaurant in the city.

Tommy went to the apartment he had bought for his grandmother and waited in the living room while his mother finished getting ready.

"I can't wait to meet her," Violet spoke to him through the closed bedroom door.

Her words surprised Tommy and he said, somewhat in jest, "Are you sure you're feeling all right?"

What was she planning?

"Yeah," Violet replied. "Why wouldn't I be? How did you meet her anyway? I don't think you ever told me."

Tommy hesitated to tell her the truth, then said, "I met her at her parents' house when I was visiting her father about business," leaving out the part about how he'd helped her out with Marie Russo.

Catherine entered the room from the kitchen, bringing Tommy a coffee. Tommy thanked her, then looked at her face to see what she thought of his mother's behavior, but Catherine just shrugged. Were they up to something? If so, what? Catherine had barely met Phoebe, except running into her once or twice when she came to see Tommy.

Violet and Catherine had reacted to the news of Phoebe's pregnancy with some shock when Tommy told them, and Catherine had congratulated him, but Violet had been quiet about it and Tommy couldn't tell what she thought.

Tommy doubted Violet or Catherine would be against his marrying Phoebe given how it would be good for business, but perhaps they planned to use the arrangement to get themselves a larger piece of the action.

"You do understand that just because Phoebe's marrying me, it doesn't mean we can just throw her family out of everything," he spoke to two of the three most important women in his life.

Catherine took him by surprise when she said, "If Pheobe's gonna be your wife, her loyalty to you should come first, above all else."

"She will be, but we can't just push them out of the neighborhood. This arrangement is about the partnership between our two families so that there will be no more trouble going forward," Tommy clarified. "Phoebe's parents, her father especially, will be a real problem if they view us as having turned against them in any way."

Violet emerged from her room, looking paler and thinner than usual, but sophisticated in her casual black dress.

"Which is why you better stay loyal to daddy's

little girl," she said with a chuckle. "I know how much you like a variety of women."

"Don't worry, I can handle it," Tommy said, sitting back on the couch.

"It's not gonna be easy for you," Violet replied.

"It certainly isn't," his grandmother commented.

Tommy hadn't considered such concerns until then. Had he planned to stay loyal to Phoebe throughout their marriage? He hadn't really thought about it. At the moment, she was the only woman in his life. In truth, he hadn't thought about his marriage as being long term. He had just assumed he'd marry Phoebe because she was sweet and pretty and it was good for his family's business, and then he'd see what happened. He never considered he might have to stay with her forever, or at least until Johnny and Camille left this world. But with a baby, he'd be tied to her always. His own father had abandoned him as a boy without so much as a second thought, and he could never do that to another child.

"I'll think of something. Don't worry about me, I'll be fine," he said to get them off his back. "It's you two I'm worried about. I don't need you interfering in any of this, causing trouble. I know how you both like to meddle."

"We won't meddle this time, Tommy," his grandmother said, with a dash of annoyance. "It'll be up to you. I'm sure you can handle it, though. Enjoy your lunch. It's a shame I wasn't invited. It would have been nice to properly meet this girl you're marrying."

"I wanted to invite you," Tommy replied. "But I wasn't sure if Phoebe could handle both of you at once. You can both be, how should I say this, overwhelming if you're in a room at the same time."

"She sounds like a nervous girl," Catherine remarked. "Is she shy?"

There were many words Tommy could use to describe Phoebe, but nervous or shy certainly weren't any of them. At least, not when they were alone. His grandmother seemed to want him to choose between her and Phoebe. He hadn't known Phoebe for as long as he'd known his grandmother, of course, but he wasn't going to speak badly of her to anyone. He genuinely cared for Phoebe, even if he wasn't in love with her entirely.

Violet touched his shoulder. "Come on, Tommy, let's go," she said, drawing him away from the tense situation.

Tommy left without answering his grandmother, and out in the hallway he thanked his mother for her support.

"She's my mother, I know how she can be sometimes. You're my son, and I'll always love you more than I love her. Don't tell her that," she added with a wink.

"How are you feeling?" Tommy asked her after a moment.

"Not bad."

"Did you remember to take your medicine?"

Violet didn't seem to like that he was playing the role of her manager. "Yes, Tommy, I did."

He left it at that.

Tommy had offered to drive Phoebe to the restaurant, but she wanted to meet them there instead. The lunch venue had valet parking, so an attendant helped with parking and Tommy left his sports car in the young man's care with a warning to be very careful with it, and promised a generous tip.

Phoebe had arrived before them, and she waved at Tommy and Violet when they entered.

"She's beautiful," Violet commented to him, eyeing Phoebe's red dress that draped over her body in a flattering way and emphasized her beautiful dark hair. "It shouldn't be too hard for you to put up with her."

Tommy noticed Phoebe's lips trembling slightly as they approached the table, and Tommy felt a little sorry for her. She was young and his mother was a formidable woman. It couldn't have been easy for her to meet them alone, and he was surprised she hadn't wanted to bring her mother along when he asked her. Then again, they were all aware of the bitter history between Camille and Violet.

"She doesn't look pregnant," Violet whispered to Tommy. "She better eat more if you want your son to be healthy."

"She just found out about the baby," Tommy replied. "I don't know if I'm having a son."

"Neither do I, but I just have this feeling you will."

"I wouldn't mind either way," Tommy answered truthfully. "They'll be mine, so I'll love them no matter what."

"I know you will." She paused. "Are you sure it's yours?"

"Jesus Christ, what kind of question is that?" Tommy snapped.

Violet shrugged. "I had to ask."

"I'm the only one Phoebe's been with, so, yeah, the kid's mine."

"She was a virgin before you met? Oh, Tommy, you don't know the trouble you're getting into. This girl is probably obsessed with you because you were her first."

"You don't know that. She isn't like that."

"I'm a woman. Believe me, I know." Violet sighed. "I don't want to argue anymore, I'm feeling tired."

Tommy looked at her with concern.

When they arrived at the table, Phoebe jumped up to shake his mother's hand.

"It's really wonderful to finally meet you," she said.

"You, too, sweetheart," Violet replied, and Phoebe blushed.

Phoebe tried to hug Violet, but his mother sat down before she could. Tommy greeted Phoebe with a kiss and whispered to her, "You're gonna be perfect."

Phoebe looked grateful and she gave him a warm smile as he sat down at her side across from his mother. There were four chairs, and Violet seemed irritated that Tommy had chosen to sit next to Phoebe instead of her. But as the father of her child and future husband, Tommy wanted to show Phoebe he supported her.

"It's great to see you out. Tommy told me how ill you were," Phoebe blurted out to his mother.

Violet merely smiled at her. She opened one of the menus that had been set out for them on the table. "Let's start with drinks," she said, putting the menu down. "Something virgin for you, of course," she said with a wink in Phoebe's direction. "Because of the baby, of course."

Phoebe's face reddened and Tommy squeezed her warm, soft hand under the table. The waiter stepped over and Violet ordered a glass of white wine, Tommy asked for a whiskey, and Phoebe wanted a lemonade drink. Tommy questioned his mother's choice.

"Are you sure that's okay with your medication?"

"Yes, Tommy, I'll be fine," she said in a resolute way.

"Tommy's talked so much about you," Phoebe told Violet, rather shyly, as they waited for their drinks to arrive.

"Has he? I hope he only said nice things about me," his mother replied.

"Oh, yes, great things," Phoebe replied quickly, although Tommy hadn't spoken to her about his mother very much, but she seemed anxious to please her.

Violet chuckled. "I was joking, sweetheart."

"Oh," Phoebe said, seeming a little crushed.

"How are you feeling?" Tommy asked Phoebe. She gave him a lovely smile. "Good, thanks."

"Are you going to a doctor regularly?" Violet

interrupted them. "It's important that you do. Babies need proper care to grow. When I was pregnant with Tommy, I saw a doctor often."

In silence, Phoebe looked at his mother in an uncertain way. Tommy had told her how social workers had removed him from his mother's care as a child due to her drug addiction.

"I'm sure Phoebe's doing everything she needs to," Tommy spoke up for the girl. "I'm sure her mother is giving her guidance."

"Camille?" Violet said with an air of distaste. "Camille's never had a baby, she has no idea what—"

Tommy stared at his mother closely and she shut up.

The waiter returned with their drinks and they sat quietly and enjoyed them for a few moments.

"Did you plan to get pregnant?" Violet suddenly asked Phoebe.

The girl looked horrified.

"When did you find out you are anyway?" Violet asked.

Tommy stared at his mother and she shrugged.

"I'm just trying to figure out the timeline of events," Violet said. "Some girls will say they're pregnant to trap a man."

"That isn't true in our case," Tommy responded, dismayed by his mother's behavior. Had she forgotten about the partnership they needed to have with Phoebe's family?

But Violet's instinct to protect her son outdid her desire for financial success.

"I would *never* do something like that," Phoebe

finally spoke up, and squeezed Tommy's hand tightly.

"All right, all right, take it easy," Violet said, looking away from her son's icy stare. "I wasn't trying to offend anyone."

"You did," Tommy responded bluntly.

They resumed having their drinks, ordered food, and the tension settled. A while later, the waiter arrived with Tommy's and Violet's sandwiches and Phoebe's salad.

"That's all you're eating?" Violet stared at Phoebe's small salad. She hadn't given her opinion earlier when Phoebe ordered. "Don't forget, you're eating for two now."

"I'm not very hungry," Phoebe replied quietly, looking down at her food.

"When I was pregnant with Tommy, I couldn't stop eating," Violet continued.

"Not every woman's like you, Ma," Tommy said to his mother, carefully. He wanted to reprimand her further, but didn't dare disrespect her in public any more than he already had. "Let's be civil and finish our meal in peace." He looked across at his mother. "Phoebe will be my wife very soon and you need to respect her."

"Of course, Tommy, no problem," Violet replied without emotion, and he couldn't tell what was really on her mind.

After they finished lunch, and Violet had had a little too much to drink, Tommy insisted on driving both Phoebe and his mother home. He tipped the attendant for taking good care of his car in his absence.

At Violet and Catherine's apartment, Tommy helped his mother inside and instructed his grandmother to keep an eye on her and give her plenty of water and strong coffee.

Phoebe waited in his car outside and he returned and closed the door behind him.

Tommy took her hand and looked into her eyes. "Phoebe, I want you to know I don't like the way my mother acted earlier in the restaurant."

"I know," she said, putting her arms around his neck. "She was just being protective of you."

"You're not pissed off? Really?"

Phoebe shook her head. "Your mother doesn't scare me, even if she scares you," she said with a smile.

Tommy chuckled. "You're a lot feistier than I realized," he told her, and he didn't think he would mind being married to her after all.

"I can't wait for you to be the father of my child," Phoebe said with a sigh, with absolute infatuation in her eyes.

CHAPTER TWENTY SEVEN

THE NEXT MORNING, Tommy apologized to his grandmother for leaving so quickly the previous afternoon by buying her flowers, which she accepted with some resistance but then gave him a smile and an embrace. Violet had acted indifferently to him ever since he scolded her at lunch, but he felt her anger would dissipate soon.

In the afternoon Tommy drove Violet and his grandmother to the pub because Violet asked to go.

"You're sure you want to go to the pub?" Tommy had asked his mother. "Even after everything that happened to you there?" After all, it was the place where she had been shot.

"I'll have to go to the pub eventually. I can't avoid it forever. I might as well get it over with," Violet had replied.

Tommy and Catherine were paying someone to manage the pub in their absence and Tommy assumed his mother wanted to see whether she approved of the manager.

Tommy parked outside the building and Violet exited the car before Tommy could insist he help her get out.

He left the car and his grandmother followed. Violet stood in front of the pub, inspecting the outside.

"The awning is looking a little tattered," she complained.

"We did the best we could," Tommy replied, trying to calm her.

"Tommy, you got more money now, you ought to take better care of the place."

"We might…" Tommy stopped short of saying, *sell it*.

"What?" Violet turned to him and asked.

"Nothing."

Although it was the family's pub, Catherine was the technical owner, and if she wanted to sell it, then that was her choice. But Tommy knew how much the pub meant to his mother, and he didn't want to break her heart so soon after she left the hospital.

Tommy and his grandmother trailed Violet inside, anticipating her next complaints. He hadn't noticed any trepidation in her movements, but, then again, his mother was a very strong woman.

The place wasn't very crowded, it never was anymore and that was one of the reasons Catherine wanted to sell it, and to their surprise Violet sat down at one of the tables in the back. Tommy asked her if she wanted to meet the manager they hired but she declined.

"Do you want a glass of wine?" Tommy asked her, wanting to help her relax.

"You're sure it's okay with my medication?" she teased him. "And since when did we start serving wine?"

"Since we needed to compete with the new places around here."

Violet nodded. "Sure, red."

Tommy went to get her the wine as his grandmother chatted with the manager. He had his back to the door and when it opened he smelled a sweet perfume. It reminded him of someone. Phoebe? No. The alluring scent reminded him of Dana's perfume. But it couldn't have been her. She was gone from his life.

Then he turned to look and Dana stood in front of him, looking as confident as ever. She was the opposite of Phoebe. They were both beautiful, but Dana had a woman's strength. Phoebe was still a girl. It struck him then how much he had once loved Dana, and he questioned his decision to marry Phoebe so soon. But with a baby on the way and his family's empire on the line, he didn't have time to think of what might have been.

"Tommy," Dana said, in her pleasant, calming voice.

"How are you?" he asked, his concern for her still strong after the ordeal he'd rescued her from.

Dana looked towards his mother's table and her face paled. "Is that—"

"It is," he answered, unsure of the outcome.

Dana's face turned red. "I don't understand. I thought she died. You lied to me."

"I didn't. I thought she died, too, that's what my grandmother told me. Everyone thought she had."

"Why did your grandmother tell you that?"

"It's a long story. She wasn't sure if my mother would recover and she wanted me to move on with my life."

"Where has your mother been all this time?"

"At a rehabilitation hospital abroad. She——"

"No, don't tell me," Dana interrupted. "It's better I don't know too much."

"Is everything okay? Why are you here?" he asked with concern, knowing what she had suffered.

"Yeah. I came to tell you something."

Violet signaled to Tommy and he asked Dana to wait one moment. He went behind the bar and poured a glass of red wine. He brought it to his mother's table.

Violet had recognized Dana immediately. "What the hell is she doing here?" she asked, motioning in Dana's direction.

"She came to see me," Tommy replied.

"Why?"

"I'm not sure. She was about to tell me."

"Get rid of her. I don't want her inside my pub. She's caused you, *us*, nothing but trouble. She's a fucking bitch."

"You don't know it, but she helped me—you—out."

"How?" Violet questioned, as though she didn't believe him.

"It's not important, but she's not a bitch."

Violet scowled at him then rolled her eyes.

Catherine had noticed Dana by then and glared

at her in silence. Dana avoided making eye contact with either of the women.

"Be nice," Tommy told his mother. "I don't think she'll be staying long."

"She better not."

"Enjoy your wine," Tommy said as he left her table.

He returned to where Dana waited by the door.

"I see your mother still hates me," Dana said, not without sarcasm.

"She doesn't."

"Oh, yeah, she does. But it's fine, I understand why."

"Do you want to sit down?" he asked her. "Have a drink?"

"No, I don't have time. I just came to see you."

"What's the rush?" Tommy asked with a smile.

She didn't return his enthusiasm. "I need to tell you something," she said, then paused. "I've decided to leave the city. I'm moving."

Tommy felt a bit sad, even though he knew it didn't make sense because he and Dana were no longer together. He looked away from her.

"Tommy?"

"I'm glad you told me," he said, facing her. "I'm not surprised to hear it," he added, which wasn't quite the truth.

"Why?"

"After what happened, it makes sense you wouldn't want to stay here. Where will you go?"

"I'm not sure. I have a friend in Canada I'm going to stay with for a while."

"Canada? That's far away. What about your

business?"

"I'm taking a little time off and then I'll start up again elsewhere."

"Oh, I see."

He hadn't planned to tell her about Phoebe and everything else, but now he knew he must.

"My girl's having a baby and we're getting married," he said.

Dana's lips trembled and for a moment Tommy thought he'd made her cry. He reached out to comfort her, but she pulled away from him.

"Who is she? Someone I know?" Dana finally spoke.

"She's Johnny and Camille Garcia's daughter. Her name's Phoebe. I don't think you know her."

Dana's expression conveyed she understood the reasons behind the marriage.

"I've never met her, no," she said quietly. "I didn't know you were with her. She must be very young." She paused. "You're going to be a father—congratulations, Tommy. I'm happy for you."

"Really?"

"Sure," she said in a thoughtful tone, but her eyes conveyed unhappiness.

"Thanks," he said. "It feels good that my life is finally back together."

"You could say that."

Tommy's brow furrowed. "What do you mean?"

"I heard about your success. So congrats on that. But, Tommy, is it the kind of success you really want?"

Her judgement roused anger in him. "You

mean, you don't approve of what I'm doing, so I shouldn't do it? Is that what you're telling me? You aren't in my life anymore, Dana, you don't get a say in what I do." He'd spoken without thinking and afterwards felt guilty for hurting her.

"I know who you used to be, and I can't believe who you are now. Camille and Johnny—getting involved with those kind of people—I'm worried about you."

Tommy laughed and saw in her eyes how much he'd disappointed her. "Don't worry about me, I'll be fine. The business I do now, it's in my family, it's part of my heritage," he said, although he knew his indifference was likely to hurt her. Then something worrying occurred to him. "What you know about me, will you keep it between us? I know you went behind my back before, so I have to ask you."

Dana frowned. "I made a mistake," she offered as though a gesture of peace. "I shouldn't have done what I did."

"Are you saying you shouldn't have helped me get fired?" he asked in surprise. "I didn't know you felt that way."

"I didn't before, but I do now. I'm sorry for what I did to you. I feel responsible for that you've become. If I hadn't said anything, then maybe—"

"Maybe I wouldn't be a gangster?"

Dana averted his gaze and nodded. It hurt to have her object to who he'd become, but he wasn't beholden to her anymore.

She looked at him closely. "No matter what happens, your secrets will always be safe with me."

"I appreciate that, Dana." They stood in silence for a moment, then Tommy said, lightly, "I hope you're not leaving the city because of me."

Dana smiled. "Don't flatter yourself," she said, and Tommy chuckled. "Goodbye, Tommy," she said, and started to walk out of the pub.

Tommy nodded but couldn't bear to watch her leaving because he knew in his heart that he'd never see her again. He looked over at his mother and grandmother who seemed to want an explanation for Dana's appearance and to hear what had transpired between them, but he went upstairs to get away from them. They'd never understand how much Dana meant to him despite her betrayal, and that, unlike them, he could never bring himself to hate her.

CHAPTER TWENTY EIGHT

VIOLET DISLIKED HOW Tommy had been a bit down ever since that Dana had visited him at the pub. He wouldn't say what Dana had wanted with him or from him, although he had clarified that it wasn't anything troublesome and that she wouldn't be visiting him again. Violet's mind filled with relief at hearing the news that Dana would be out of her son's life forever, as the less Tommy saw of that woman, the better.

Now Tommy was asking her to come together with Camille to prepare for his upcoming wedding to Pheobe. In private, she'd wanted to knock her son over the head for getting that girl pregnant and basically being forced to marry her. Then again, it would be good for business, and Violet liked anything that helped the family business.

The wedding, a small event, would be held at the country house of Camille's mother Sheila and her mob lawyer husband, Aldo. Violet wasn't very happy that Camille's family had more control over the event, but they were the family of the bride, and at the same time she also took comfort in the fact that Tommy's wealth was growing.

But when Tommy asked her to go shopping with Camille for decorations, she'd almost passed out.

"You want me to do *what*?"

"Go visit a few shops with her, pick out a few nice things for the wedding. It's what the mothers of the bride and groom traditionally do together."

Tommy had stopped by Violet and Catherine's apartment with his request, which he'd presented to her after she'd made him coffee.

Still feeling a little weak, Violet sat down on the living room couch.

"You do know the history between me and that woman, don't you?" she said, looking up at him.

Tommy sat next to her and patted her hand. "I know you don't want to go and I know why that is, but Pheobe and I will be wife and husband soon, and you're gonna have to get along with her family or at least pretend you do." He drank his coffee.

"Tommy, when I was in the hospital and I told you about my plans to make a deal with that family, I didn't mean you should get so involved with them, I didn't mean you should marry their daughter, for fuck's sake."

"I know, but it just happened."

"It just happened? It didn't just happen. It happened because you couldn't keep your dick in your pants around that girl, that's how it happened."

"I proposed to her before I knew she was having a baby. Her parents found out about us and I knew they'd be pissed because she was so young. I didn't want anything to get in the way of the partnership, so I asked her to marry me."

Violet shook her head. "You should've stayed away from her."

"She kept coming to see me."

"Of course she did."

"Ma, I'm not asking you to move in with her family, I'm just asking you to go shopping with her mother for a few hours. You don't even have to talk to her that much, just be pleasant."

Violet laughed. "Pleasant to that bitch? You're lucky if I don't strangle her. Trust me, Tommy, you do not want to leave me alone with her."

"But you said yourself you planned to make a truce with her."

"Yeah, but I never said I'd go shopping with her. Whose idea was this, anyway? Yours or your girl's?"

"It's traditional," Tommy said. "We both want you to go. You're gonna have to learn to be polite to Phoebe's family."

"I'll be polite to Camille, I just don't want to talk to her or go shopping with her."

"Come on, Ma, I'm asking you to do this for me," he said, giving her one of his charming smiles, because she knew that he knew she couldn't resist him when he showed her affection.

"Oh, fine, I'll go. It's fucking crazy, and I'm only doing it for you, but I'll spend some time with that bitch."

"Thanks, Ma," he said, giving her another smile.

"Just don't call her a bitch to her face."

"Don't you worry," Violet said, stroking his face. "I'll be able to control myself. I think," she laughed.

Violet was still a little tired, and Catherine helped her dress fashionably and Tommy drove her to the shopping center to meet Camille.

"I'll walk you in," he said, and started to open his door.

"No, I'll be fine on my own," Violet replied, opening her door.

"You're sure?"

"Tommy, I'm your mother. I don't need an escort. I'm not a child," she stated firmly.

But ever since returning from the hospital it seemed like Tommy had started to think of her as someone who needed his constant protection instead of the formidable woman she had once been.

"Ma, it's no problem, I'm happy to—"

"Tommy, no." Violet got out and shut the door. She waved goodbye to him through the window.

Tommy knew better than to go against her wishes so he stayed inside the car, and when Violet turned around, he waved at her again then drove away.

It didn't take long for Violet to notice Camille Garcia. Camille O'Brien, as she had been known as when they'd first met many years ago. Guided by a cane, Camille entered the shopping center ahead of her. Camille's need for a cane was a direct result of when Violet shot her, although Camille had also done her part to maim Violet at the time.

So, in a way, Violet guessed they were even, but Camille had been left with more noticeable scars.

Violet paused before going inside, deciding how she might approach Camille. She hoped Camille would make an initial gesture as she didn't want to be the first one. After a few moments of reminding herself she was only going through with this for Tommy, Violet entered and quickly looked around. Inside the building were many expensive shops to choose from.

Camille turned around and stood in the middle of Violet's path, leaving Violet unable to avoid her.

Relief relaxed Violet's entire body when Camille spoke first.

"My daughter asked me to come here."

"Tommy wanted me to come as well," Violet replied.

"Or else there's no chance in hell we'd be here, right?" Camille surprised her with a smile.

Unwilling to give into Camille's gesture, Violet just nodded. While they were both guilty of shooting the other during the same incident, the way Violet figured it, Camille had done worse to her in the long run. Not only had she ruined Violet's family's crime dynasty many years ago, but Camille also had her own mother beat the shit out of her, then blamed Violet and got her arrested for the crime. Thankfully, Camille's plan hadn't worked and the truth emerged.

"Let me make this clear straightaway," she told Camille now. "Our kids are getting married and my son is working with your family now, but we ain't ever gonna be friends."

"You letting Tommy run things these days?" Camille questioned, with a glimmer of defiance in her eyes.

Violet hadn't given the situation much consideration after her release from the hospital. She didn't like not being involved when it came to matters of the family business, but she had always planned to hand control over to Tommy when he was ready, which she felt he was. She wasn't going to take a back seat, however, and still wanted some say.

But she knew how to get Camille where it would hurt her the most. "That's what happens when you have a son, you hand him the family business. That's something you wouldn't understand."

Of course, part of the reason Violet had accepted Tommy's marriage to Phoebe was that since Camille and Johnny had no sons, Violet envisioned Tommy controlling the entire empire someday.

Camille's defiant expression faded and, for once, she seemed not to know how to respond. Camille had her stepdaughter Phoebe, but Violet knew Camille couldn't have children and that was something she'd always have over her. Violet knew she had hurt her badly, but she didn't apologize.

Camille shook her head, then started laughing, shocking Violet.

"Even after all this time, and with our children about to get married, you're still such a fucking bitch," Camille said, but Violet didn't react.

"Being in a coma hasn't changed you at all, Violet. How are you feeling, anyway? You don't seem to have any memory problems, that's for sure."

"I feel fine, actually," Violet replied coolly, when she still felt a little weak. "I got no issues." She eyed Camille's cane.

Camille shook her head, again. "I don't like you, Violet. I never have and I'm sure I never will. But your son seems like a good man, and he's gonna marry my daughter, so I will tolerate you. Can you tolerate me?"

Camille seemed willing to let bygones be bygones. In Violet's absence, Camille had morphed into a matronly figure and had become someone unfamiliar to Violet. Violet still disliked Camille, but, in a way, she had to admire the other woman's sense.

Violet glared at her then nodded in silence.

"Come on, we have some shopping for decorations to do," Camille broke the tension. "My Phoebe wants a lot of nice things." She began to walk ahead of Violet, albeit slowly, with her cane clacking on the floor.

Violet caught up with her. "I'm paying," she stated.

Camille and Johnny were paying for most of the wedding, but Violet wasn't about to let them get away with paying for everything, especially now that Tommy had plenty of money.

Camille stopped in her tracks and faced her. "The family of the bride pays, that's how it's always done. I said I was willing to tolerate you, but I will not have you controlling this wedding."

"I'm not controlling anything, I'm paying for the damn decorations."

"You know, Violet, as I said before, you haven't changed at all from when I first met you all those years ago. When Phoebe told me what Tommy said about you considering a partnership with us before you were shot, I thought maybe you had changed. But you haven't, not at all."

"I don't know what Tommy told you, but whatever I told him when I was in the hospital can't be taken seriously as I was still coming out of my coma," she lied.

"You're saying your son lied to us?"

Violet didn't want to jeopardize Tommy's plans so she rushed to rectify the situation. "He didn't lie."

"So, you did say it?" Camille challenged.

"I don't know what I said exactly. I was still recovering, but if Tommy says I did say it, then I must've said something along those lines, yeah. Tommy wouldn't lie to you."

Camille smiled knowingly, and Violet practically shook with rage as she imagined the enjoyment Camille felt from the hold she had over her.

"Phoebe told me what happened when she went to lunch with you and Tommy," Camille said. "You ought to own up to that, too."

"I don't know what you're talking about," Violet shot back, when she very much did remember.

Camille smirked. "Oh, I think you do. You insulted my daughter."

"I didn't insult anyone. I asked a few questions about the timing of everything. I never said

Tommy wasn't the father."

"You said she could be lying about being pregnant," Camille snapped at her.

"I wanted clarification, that's all."

"Bullshit."

"I was looking out for my son. I'm sure you'd do the same for your Phoebe."

"Phoebe is a good, sweet girl. She'd never tell such a lie!"

"I'm sure she didn't," Violet said to defuse the situation although she still had her doubts.

"You better be sure."

"Forget I said anything. But I'm still paying for the decorations," Violet clarified.

Camille rolled her eyes. "This is gonna be a long day."

CHAPTER TWENTY NINE

PHOEBE SAT BY the window in her apartment at night, looking out at the iridescent lights of the vast city. She quietly drank a glass of red wine alone. There was no baby to worry about.

She'd lied to everyone. She couldn't risk losing Tommy. Ever since she first saw him at her parents' house, being with him was constantly on her mind. Phoebe considered herself a strong young woman, but she was infatuated with him in a way she had never been with anyone else. Her desire for him made her crazy.

It wasn't just because he was the first man who'd successfully seduced her. Everything about Tommy drew her in, from his looks and charisma to his voice and the way he carried himself. Besides her father, no other man had protected her and made her feel so safe. Phoebe couldn't forget how Tommy had been the only person willing to help her out with the Marie situation and she couldn't imagine herself being without him.

But although Tommy was a good man, he was

still very much a man, and with his nice looks, power, and money, Phoebe knew he had plenty of options, and the question of whether he'd agreed to marry her in the first place only to appease her father and would somehow find a way to back out of the arrangement, weighed on her mind ever since he'd proposed to her. After all, she had put Tommy in a position where he couldn't say no. She wasn't thinking of the long term and she knew she couldn't force him to stay in their marriage forever, but a baby would ensure that he'd at least go through with the wedding.

Phoebe herself was the only one who knew about the lie. So far. But what would she do when no baby came and Tommy started to ask questions? She could say she suffered a miscarriage when the time came, although that risked destroying him emotionally. Or she could find a baby.

Phoebe finished her wine, rose, and hide the bottle in the trash.

———◆———

Tommy spent the next morning overseeing the renovations to his new nightclub. He planned to turn the place into an upscale lounge with beautiful waitresses dressed in not much clothing and cocktails with high prices and names with international appeal. The drinks didn't even have to be high quality, as Tommy found that if you gave something a fancy name and charged more for it, more people longed for it.

The neighborhood was changing fast and

Tommy saw great opportunity in such a venture. He felt some sadness, too, that the neighborhood's old way of life, its rich past which included his own family's history, was disappearing, but the chance to increase his own success made those feelings disappear. His grandmother was partly right about them not needing the old pub anymore, but his mother had such a strong attachment to the place, he couldn't bear to cause her pain so soon after her ordeal. In a way, he'd come to agree with his grandmother about the pub, but to protect his mother's heart he'd never tell his grandmother his true feelings.

The men who Tommy had hired to modernize the club were local builders he knew from growing up in the neighborhood. As boys, Tommy had been one of them, bantering and playing in the streets, getting into all sorts of trouble. But now they viewed him as the boss, as someone above them. Now they didn't make small talk or joke with him, they feared him. It was then that Tommy realized how much his power had grown and how vast his hold over the neighborhood had become.

As he went over the plans for the glass and marble bar, Phoebe walked inside, looking as fresh and gorgeous as ever. The workmen avoided looking at her, although Tommy assumed they wanted to, as she was so beautiful, but Tommy radiated an animalistic vibe whenever around Phoebe as though he'd maim anyone who caused her any slight discomfort. Especially now that she was carrying his child. The baby had changed

Tommy's perspective of everything. He had to protect Phoebe at all costs. Their child would be his legacy, and Tommy knew that any child of his would become a target of his enemies, as would Phoebe herself.

Phoebe touched Tommy's hand and kissed him lightly on his face. She smelled very sweet.

"How are you?" she asked him. "The place is looking amazing." She cast a glance over the club's evolving interior.

"Is everything okay?" he replied, although it wasn't unusual for her to stop by for a visit.

"Yeah, I felt like seeing you."

"How are you feeling?" he asked.

"Fine," Phoebe said, after a few seconds.

But why had she hesitated to answer him?

"Are you taking proper care of yourself?" he asked her in concern.

"Yes, I'm following everything my doctor tells me. You never were so concerned about me before, Tommy," she said, but he could tell she enjoyed the new attention he gave her. "I'm not sure if it's me or the baby you really want."

"I want you both," he said, grabbing her and pulling her close to him, challenging her with his gaze.

Phoebe turned away from him as he held her. "I hope I'm enough for you, Tommy."

He touched her face and made her look at him. "Of course you are." He let her go and gestured around them. "This will be our son's someday."

"Or daughter's."

"Yes, or our daughter's. When can we find out

what we're having?" he asked, eager for news.

"Tommy, you know I don't want to know before I have the baby."

"If we know, we can plan better."

Phoebe ignored him and he grabbed her by the arm.

"What's wrong?" he asked. "What's going on with you? There's something you're not telling me."

"No!" Phoebe shouted, pulling away from him. "Nothing's wrong." Then she dared to say, "Our child will be more than someone to pass your business onto."

Anger rose from within him. "What did you say to me?"

"I didn't mean anything by it," she quickly, but faintly, replied.

It took a lot of strength for him not to slap her. Tommy left for a moment to cool off. He spoke with some of the workmen, then returned to Phoebe and decided to use a softer approach.

"Phoebe, what are you not telling me?"

She shrugged, then when he wouldn't stop staring at her, she said, "I've had this feeling lately, an uneasy feeling."

Right away, he knew what she meant. "About Marie Russo?"

Phoebe looked down and nodded. "Marie's one of the things bothering me."

"She's in jail and my sources say she'll be there for a very long time. Her father isn't helping her and her mother doesn't have enough cash to get her out. You got your revenge, baby." He gave her a wink, then paused. "You said Marie is one of the things on your mind. What's the other?"

"Nothing important," she replied.

"You're sure?"

Phoebe nodded.

"I can send someone, one of our guys, to be with you during the times when I can't be, to make sure you feel safe. I wouldn't want anything to happen to the baby."

Phoebe frowned. "And me?"

"And you, of course. I'll send someone to be with you." He started to call one of the large men who worked for him over to where they stood.

Phoebe stopped him. "No, that's not needed. Please don't worry," she said, with a smile, and kissed his cheek. After a moment, she said, "Let's have more than one child. Let's have lots of kids."

Tommy smiled and nodded to appease her, but the way he saw it, the more children they had, the more he had to lose, as any child of his would become a target of his enemies.

Phoebe sensed the change in his mood. "What's the matter?" she asked.

"Nothing," Tommy replied, pulling her close to his side. "You and me, we're gonna have a great life."

"We'll be king and queen of this city someday very soon," she said, looking up at him and grinning, her beautiful teeth gleaming in the dim nightclub.

"You sound like Camille, you sound like your ma."

"Is that a bad thing?"

"No. I just never thought of you as being like her."

"I am like her, in some ways. I'm just as ambitious as she is, you know."

"I don't doubt it." Tommy looked at her closely and winked.

———◆———

Tommy seemed to sense Phoebe's troubles and it alarmed her. He hadn't questioned the baby's existence, exactly, unlike his meddlesome mother, but would any lingering doubts lead him to not go through with the wedding? Phoebe knew that their marriage was vital to the success of each of their family's businesses, but Tommy was a proud man, and if he discovered she'd fooled him, who knew what he might do?

After visiting Tommy at his nightclub, Phoebe bought a simple chocolate cake from the bakery near her apartment and took the train to her parents' house in the suburbs when she knew her father would be out at the gym for the afternoon and her mother would be alone.

Camille didn't seem surprised to see her.

"Phoebe, I expected you would come to see me," she said when she greeted Phoebe at the front door.

"Why?"

"Your father's not here, which you already know. Something's been off about you lately. I can always tell when something's on my baby's mind." Camille's eyes drifted to the cake box in Phoebe's hands. "Is that for me?" she said with a smile. "Oh, sweetheart you shouldn't have, but thank you."

Phoebe handed the box to her. "I know how much you like chocolate cake."

"Is this to sweeten me up before you tell me some bad news?" Camille asked, seeing right through her.

"How did you know?" Phoebe asked, her face getting hot.

"Oh, sweetheart, I know you very well."

Phoebe entered all the way and Camille closed the door.

"Come into the kitchen and we'll have some of this cake you brought me," Camille said as she walked away. "I'm sure it's delicious."

Phoebe stood in place and started crying. Camille stopped walking, set down the cake box, and ran back to her.

Phoebe had come to think of Camille as her mother over the years and she trusted her with all her heart.

"Phoebe, what the hell is going on with you?" Camille asked. "Did Tommy do something to upset you?"

Her first instinct was to defend him. "No, it's nothing he did. Tommy's been wonderful to me," she said, which was true. Mostly.

"He bought you a huge ring. Now you're getting married in a few days. What do you have to be so upset about?"

She had already been fitted for a stunning, elaborate dress and many generous wedding gifts had started to arrive at her parents' house. The people her family did business with and those from her parents' old neighborhood all wanted to make a good impression on the couple.

Camille's face paled. "Is it the baby? Is something wrong with the baby?"

Unable to look at her step-mother, Phoebe covered her face with her hands and sobbed.

"Phoebe, what's wrong with the baby?" Camille grabbed her arm and shook her out of it.

Phoebe pulled away and screamed, "There is no baby!"

Camille's eyes reddened as though she was on the verge of crying. "You lost the baby?"

Phoebe knew how much a grandchild would mean to her step-mother. She shook her head. "There never was a baby. I lied. I lied to everyone. I'm sorry." She tried to embrace Camille, but her step-mother pushed her away.

"You lied?" she shouted.

"I'm sorry," Phoebe pleaded, unable to control the warm tears flowing down her face. "What am I going to do? I need to tell Tommy." She sobbed hysterically. Not thinking, she started to leave the house. "I'm going to tell Tommy."

Camille grabbed her and pulled her back inside. "Control yourself, girl. You can never tell him. He won't want to go through with the wedding if you do and he'll hate you forever. It'll destroy the partnership your father and I have worked so hard to make with him and his family. We need that partnership. I don't want any more wars, I'm too fucking old for them!"

Phoebe knew just how vital her marriage to

Tommy was for her family's success, and as much as she was absolutely infatuated with Tommy, she also wanted to marry him to please her stepmother.

Phoebe stopped crying and Camille cleaned her face with a tissue.

"I don't know what to do," Phoebe said. "I don't know how I'm going to get out of this."

"Why did you do it in the first place? He already wanted to marry you. You already had him."

"I didn't want to lose him! Everything happened so fast and I knew he'd been pressured into asking me to marry him. I thought he might back out before the wedding."

"Phoebe, you're acting crazy. He wouldn't have backed out. He needs to be on our good side."

"And he loves me," Phoebe added.

"Yes, there's that, too," Camille replied, although she didn't sound as sure.

"I love him so much. I didn't want to lose him. I *can't* lose him."

"You're obsessed, it isn't healthy."

"You don't think he feels the same way about me?" Phoebe began to panic, though on the inside, she'd wondered the same thing since the start.

"Has he told you he loves you?"

"No, but it's different for men. They don't say it as much. I know you and Dad are unique in that you both say it all the time to each other, but you aren't like most couples."

Camille looked like she didn't approve of Phoebe's way of thinking.

"You don't believe me?" Phoebe asked, her body warming from frustration.

"I won't say anything more," Camille told her resolutely. "I will say that I was crazy about your father when we were young, so I can understand your intense feelings. You are my daughter, Phoebe, and I will support you no matter what. But what I'm going to tell you will sound harsh, but I have to say it. You fucked up big time, sweetheart, and you can't keep doing things like this or else you're gonna hurt our family. You know the business we're in, you know how fragile these partnerships are. All it takes is one person to ruin it all. Don't be that person, Phoebe."

"Are you threatening me?" Phoebe asked, and took a step back.

"No, of course not," Camille said, reaching towards her. "I just want you to be careful. We all have to be careful. We're not going to hurt you. I'd never hurt you. But others might."

It took a few moments for Phoebe to believe her. "I came to you because I knew I could trust you."

"More than your father?"

"I trust you both, but you know how he gets. You're calmer than him. Will you help me, Ma?"

"It's so nice to hear you call me your ma."

"I should've done it more when I was growing up. You've become my ma, you *are* my ma."

Camille wrapped her arms around Phoebe and held her tightly. "Of course I'll help you, sweetheart." Then Camille chuckled.

Phoebe looked at her. "What's so funny?"

"I was just thinking how I yelled at Violet for accusing you of lying about the baby and she was right after all. I never thought I'd say this, but I owe her an apology. But I wouldn't apologize to that woman if she held a knife to my throat."

"I know you don't like her, but I love her son."

"I know you do, sweetheart. Don't worry, I won't cause trouble. I might want to, but, for you, I will resist."

"Oh, Ma. What the hell am I going to do about this baby?" Pheobe said with a sigh.

"We'll figure it out when the time comes," Camille spoke with confidence.

"Will you tell Dad?" Phoebe asked with concern.

"I can't lie to him."

"No, please don't tell him!" Phoebe begged.

"He's my husband, he's your father, I can't lie to him!"

"Please," Phoebe pleaded, staring intently at Camille. Overwhelmed by the idea of her father discovering her dishonesty, her lips began to quiver and more tears appeared.

Camille stroked Phoebe's face and her touch felt calming. "Hush now, I won't say anything to anyone," she promised.

"Not even Dad?"

"Not even him."

CHAPTER THIRTY

O N THE DATE of the wedding, the weather
was warm and sunny, and the marriage ceremony seemed destined to be a beautiful event.
Tommy drove alone to the country house of
Sheila and Aldo, about an hour from the city.
Phoebe had wanted them to go there together,
but Tommy insisted that would break with tradition. The event would have minimal guests,
just Sheila and Aldo, and Camille and Johnny on
Phoebe's side, and Violet and Catherine on his.
There were to be no best man for him or brides-
maids for Phoebe, as they hadn't had enough
time to plan for those.

Tommy arrived and walked to the house. There
were already cars there, and for a moment he fretted that he had somehow lost track of the time
and was late. But when he checked his watch, he
was right on time.

Tommy had never been to Sheila and Aldo's
large stone manor before, but Phoebe had told
him its history and how well Aldo had done for
himself as a lawyer representing some of the most
prominent mobsters in the city. The home had

vast, well-maintained colorful gardens surrounding it, and seemed like the perfect place for a wedding.

The priest, who Tommy knew from the city, an older, white-haired man who was loyal to both families, had already arrived and chatted with Tommy's grandmother, dressed elegantly, near a white-flower-strewn arch where Phoebe and Tommy would stand under to recite their vows during the outdoor ceremony. There hadn't been enough time to hire a wedding planner, but Violet and Camille had selected lovely decorations for the ceremony, fancy, embellished pieces. Some glittered and shone in the sunlight.

His grandmother noticed his presence and stepped away from the priest to greet him.

"Tommy, you look so handsome in your tuxedo," she said, opening her arms to embrace her.

He held her close to him and she smelled like lavender.

"I have to say," Catherine told him, "At first, I wasn't happy about this wedding happening, but seeing you here, showing up on time, all dressed up, has changed my mind. I think this will be good for you, Tommy. Not just for the family business, but for your heart as well. You've been through a lot of terrible things over the years, especially that bitch betraying you, and I think Phoebe's gonna be good for you. I can tell she really loves you."

Tommy started to tell her that Dana had apologized to him, but a burst of concern filled his mind and he released his grandmother and looked at her. "Yeah, but having a kid? What kind of father am I gonna be? I didn't have a real father. What if I fuck it up?"

"You're not gonna fuck it up. You're gonna be a great father. Having a child is a beautiful thing. Trust me, I know." She looked to the distance and smiled and seemed to be thinking of Violet. "You will do well."

"Yeah, but bringing a kid into this world, our kind of world, you know the risks. Something bad could happen to them because of who we are."

"You mean, someone might try to hurt them to get to you?"

Tommy nodded.

"That could happen," Catherine admitted, not heartlessly. "But that's just how we live our lives. You can't think about it too much or else you won't survive."

What if he couldn't protect Phoebe? What if he couldn't protect their child?

"I can't not think about it," Tommy replied.

"You'll learn to. I know from experience." She paused. "Don't let this ruin today. People will notice if you're fretting."

"Have you seen Phoebe?" he asked, suddenly having an urge to check on her.

"I have. But you can't. Remember? It's bad luck."

"Right," Tommy said.

Phoebe was somewhere hidden away from him and he'd have to wait to see her when everyone else did.

"Do you think she's safe?" he asked.

"Of course! Why wouldn't she be? She's with her mother. Did something happen?" Catherine's eyes narrowed in concern.

"No," Tommy replied. "She came to me a while ago and said she felt uneasy."

"About what?"

"I'm not sure, she wouldn't say."

"It's probably nothing. Pre-wedding nerves or something like that." She paused. "I have some news to tell you."

Tommy waited for her to elaborate.

"I've decided to drop the idea of selling the pub," she said. "As long as I'm alive. Then I'll leave it up to you and your mother."

"Ma would be happy to hear that, but she doesn't know. I never said anything to her. Did you?"

Catherine shook her head.

"It'll be our secret, then," Tommy said. "She won't take it well if she thinks we went behind her back about the pub."

"Our secret. I won't say anything."

"How do you think Ma's doing, anyway? I was skeptical at first, but her memory seems fine."

"She's doing well, I wouldn't worry. It's nothing short of a miracle considering everything that's happened. It's not easy for her to hand over control to you, but she's adjusting. It's a tradition so she knows that's how it has to be. She's proud of you, and I know my father would be proud of you also."

Tommy thanked his grandmother. His mother,

who was speaking with Sheila's husband, at the other side of the garden, waved at him.

"I didn't know she was friends with Aldo," Tommy remarked to his grandmother, indicating at Violet and Sheila's husband.

"Not friends, but she can stand him. Unlike her relationship with his step-daughter." His grandmother paused, then said, "I had a thought."

"What is it?"

"It's about your mother and Camille. You don't think they'll kill each other during the ceremony, do you?"

"You're joking?"

Catherine shook her head.

"They're never gonna be friends," Tommy said. "But they managed to go shopping together and both returned alive. So I don't think they'll kill each other. At least not yet," he added, and they both chuckled.

"Come here, give me another hug," Catherine said, and reached for him. She patted his back and said, "I am so proud of the man you've become."

———◆———

The day before Phoebe's wedding her life changed in the most unexpected way. She awoke in the morning feeling unwell and her mother encouraged her to see a doctor when they spoke on the phone. She couldn't afford to be ill during her wedding the next day. Her doctor ran a few tests, then asked her if it was possible she was pregnant. Phoebe had nearly cried at his question then replied, "If you only knew the whole story."

Regardless, he ran another test.

And it came back positive.

She *was* having a baby. Phoebe couldn't believe it. At first, she thought the doctor must have somehow been wrong, but he showed her the results on paper. And when she asked him if they could tell whether the child was a boy or a girl, because although she had told Tommy she didn't wish to know, she really did, the doctor ran another test. She'd hurried home with the results to prepare for her wedding.

But she hadn't told anyone, not even the one person who knew her secret. She hadn't told Camille.

On her wedding day, Phoebe sat in the guest bedroom at Granny Sheila's country house as Camille applied makeup to her and styled her hair. Phoebe had wanted to hire a professional stylist, but Camille insisted on doing it herself. Ever since Phoebe had been kidnapped, her step-mother didn't seem to trust strangers entering Phoebe's life in any way, no matter how small.

Phoebe sat and watched in the mirror as Camille worked on her, waiting for the perfect moment to reveal her news. Her wedding gown was draped over the bed, ready for her to put on.

"I never thought your wedding day would come so soon," Camille said. "I always figured you'd get married, but never so young."

"I'll always be your and Dad's little girl." Phoebe looked up at her and smiled.

"I know," Camille said, stroking her hair with the brush. "Have you thought about what you told me the other day? Ignoring it won't make it better. I have some ideas—"

"No," Phoebe interrupted her, and Camille stopped brushing her hair.

"What is it, Phoebe? What's going on?" Camille asked. "You didn't tell Tommy your secret, did you? He's not gonna show up if you did."

"That's not it. That's not it at all. Remember how yesterday I said I wasn't feeling well and you told me to see my doctor?"

"Yeah. I should've called you after your appointment to see how you were, but I was so busy with the wedding arrangements. Are you ill? You don't look ill." Camille stared at her in the mirror.

"Not exactly. But there is something going on with me," Phoebe replied, unable to contain her smile.

"Don't keep me waiting, Phoebe. Tell me!" Camille dropped the brush to the floor in frustration. "Are you dying? Why are you smiling like that?"

"No! It turns out I'm not ill, I'm pregnant."

"What? Phoebe, that's crazy. Don't lie to me." She looked at her sternly.

"I'm not lying. Here's the paperwork to prove it." Phoebe removed the paper with the initial results from her purse on the table at her side.

Camille grabbed it from her and read. "Is this fake? Where did you buy this? Who sold it to you? Tell me their names and I'll find them! I'll kill the bastards."

"I didn't buy it from anyone. It's real. The doctor gave it to me. You've met my doctor. According to him, I'm having a baby."

"How is this possible?"

"Well, I did sleep with Tommy," Phoebe said quietly.

"That's not what I meant," Camille sounded frustrated. "I mean, you weren't pregnant when you told everyone you were and now you are. How can you be so lucky?"

Phoebe shrugged. "I haven't thought about it, I'm just relieved."

"I bet you are. I still can't believe it."

"Ma, stop. It's real."

"Next thing you know you'll be finding out you're having a boy!" Camille beamed.

"I am," Phoebe giggled.

"What?" Camille practically screamed.

"I asked the doctor to check. It's a boy."

Camille grinned. "Oh, Phoebe, you are one fucking lucky girl." She put her arm around Phoebe's shoulders and embraced her. "My beautiful, lucky girl, on her wedding day." She smiled at Phoebe in the mirror.

Camille grabbed the brush from the floor and started styling Phoebe's hair again. "You should name the baby after your dad or my father."

"Tommy will probably want to name it after himself," Phoebe replied. "Or after his dad."

"Just don't name him after Tommy's great-grandfather…never mind. Today is gonna be a beautiful day," Camille said, as though she didn't want to involve Phoebe in the past. "There are lots of distinguished names out there."

"He'll also have a middle name, too, you know,"

Phoebe added with a smile. Then she sighed. "I don't know if I can lie to Tommy forever. After we're married I'm going to tell him the truth. That's what I plan to do. I'm going to tell him I wasn't really pregnant until later. I can't live with the lie. I'd feel so guilty."

"Never feel guilty about anything. That's how you survive in our world as a woman." Camille abruptly stopped working on Phoebe's hair and walked around to face her. "You can *never* tell him, Phoebe, or else he'll hate you forever." She shook the brush at her.

"He won't," Phoebe insisted, pulling away. "Tommy's not like that."

"Listen to me. He *is* like that. You don't know men like I do, you're nearly still a child."

"But I know Tommy. I know what he's like—"

"No. You'll lose him if you tell him and you'll never get him back. It's better to keep lying to him."

Phoebe hesitated and then looked up at Camille and asked quietly, "Do you lie to Dad?"

"Of course not, our marriage isn't like that," Camille answered with a frown. She resumed shaping Phoebe's hair.

"Then why should I lie to my husband?" Phoebe questioned.

"Because your marriage will be different. Too much is at stake."

"You mean, too much is at stake for you and Dad," Phoebe mumbled.

Camille froze. "This is serious, Phoebe. This isn't some little game. I mean what I said. You can never tell Tommy. We don't know how he'll react, what he'll do. We can't trust him."

"Can't trust him? I'm getting married to him in a few moments, for fuck's sake!"

Camille seemed startled by her swearing, which she rarely did in front of her parents.

"That's just how women like us have to live our lives," Camille replied.

"But you said you and Dad weren't like that."

"Your father is unique." She paused. "Listen to me, Phoebe. Do as I say and you'll be fine." She smiled at Phoebe and seemed to be trying to encourage her. "Today is your big day so let's not discuss this again. Let's think of brighter things."

Phoebe nodded at Camille and managed a smile. But fear and uncertainty filled her heart. She'd felt Tommy would be there for her no matter what happened and inside her soul she believed he could forgive her for her dishonesty, but she'd known Camille forever and didn't think she would ever lie to her, so perhaps her desire for transparency had been unwise.

"I won't say anything to him," she promised Camille faintly.

CHAPTER THIRTY ONE

———

PLEASANT, RECORDED MUSIC played in the background as Phoebe walked towards Tommy in her elaborate, silk and lace wedding gown, escorted by her father, looking so beautiful and precious, and innocent. Tommy stood waiting for her under the decorated arch with the priest behind him. He could feel his mother's and grandmother's eyes on him from where they sat at the other side of Camille, Sheila, and Aldo.

Watching Phoebe approaching him with such grace and courage, and her veil showing a tiny, mischievous smile intended only for him, made Tommy realize he could love Phoebe. Someday, if not yet. He found he didn't want to flee and disappear, he decided he would go through with the wedding. Not just for his family's sake, but because being married to a girl like Phoebe could be a lot of fun, and after all the terrible shit Tommy had endured in his still relatively young life, he deserved to have a little fun.

As Phoebe's father handed her off to Tommy at the arch, he gave him a firm look that said, 'She may be yours now, but she'll always be mine. You better not ever hurt her'. Tommy acknowledged him with a nod. Then Johnny returned to his seat.

Tommy towered over Phoebe as she stood closely next to him in front of the priest. The man smiled at the couple and began the ceremony. Tommy could feel Phoebe shaking from nerves alongside him and he turned his head very slightly and gave her a wink only she could see. She suppressed a giggle and he saw her blushing under her veil.

As they each said, "I do," and exchanged rings, and Tommy removed Phoebe's veil and leaned in to kiss her, everyone watching rose and clapped their hands.

Tommy began kissing Phoebe's soft, full lips, when a woman's voice he didn't recognize started shouting. Was someone trying to stop the wedding? One of his scorned former lovers, perhaps? The voice didn't sound like Dana's. He stopped kissing Phoebe and they both turned to see what was going on.

A woman he didn't know, older, tall, with dark good looks, dressed much too casually to be an unexpected wedding guest, bolted down the aisle.

"Who the hell is that?" Tommy muttered.

Johnny quickly rose to stop the woman, but she pushed him off her and grabbed a gun from her pocket. She stopped when she reached Tommy and Phoebe.

"What the fuck do you think you're doing, you crazy bitch? This is our wedding!" Tommy screamed at her, not caring a priest was nearby.

"She's the one I came for!" the woman shouted,

pointing the gun in Phoebe's direction. "She doesn't know who I am, but I sure as hell know who she is. This little bitch ruined my Marie's life!"

"You're Marie's mother?" Tommy asked in shock.

She nodded. "Isabella," she said her name.

"How the fuck did you get in here?"

"I sneaked through the back side of the estate." Isabella waved the gun at Phoebe. "She started the fire that ruined my daughter's shop and that's how the police found the coke. Now my Marie's in fucking jail because of this bitch."

"Don't fucking talk to my wife that way," Tommy cautioned. "I was the one who ordered your daughter's fucking shop to be burned down, you stupid bitch."

"You did it for her then," Isabella yelled.

"Tommy, is this true?" Violet asked him from the audience.

He didn't answer her.

"I've been following you," Isabella said to Phoebe. "I've been asking around about you. It's amazing what some people will tell you for a little cash."

They hadn't been very open about the wedding's location for security reasons, and Tommy's mind raced with thoughts of who had betrayed them. He vowed to find and brutally deal with those who had.

"Marie's father Vito disowned her because of you. You took Marie's happiness, so now I'm gonna take yours!" Isabella screamed.

What happened next seemed to occur in slow motion. Isabella aimed the gun at Phoebe, and her eyes burned so intently with anger that Tommy knew she would shoot Phoebe. The priest moved out of the way. Tommy couldn't lose Phoebe and his child and watch it happen. He jumped in between the two women as Isabella fired the gun and threw himself over Phoebe, taking her to the ground with him.

Afterwards, he didn't know himself if he'd been shot. His eyes were closed and it took him a moment to assess if he felt any pain. His head hurt like hell from the abrupt drop to the ground, but he'd managed to cushion Phoebe's fall.

Johnny tackled Isabella to the ground and Camille and Violet pinned her down.

Phoebe knelt over Tommy, clinging to him and shouting his name. Then his mother called to him. Tommy opened his eyes and managed to move onto his side. He felt his body for signs of an injury, and when he found none, he grabbed Phoebe and stood up with her cradling his arms.

She embraced him tightly and buried her face in his chest. Her tears wet his shirt.

"I thought I'd lost you," she whispered. "Why the hell did you do that? Do you know how close you came to being killed?" She gestured to the arch behind them that had a bullet pierced through it.

"I couldn't lose you," he replied with a smile. "Let's finish what we started," he said, and kissed her.

"Well, that was interesting," the priest commented from where he stood near Tommy and Phoebe. "Congratulations," he told the couple. The usually stern man managed a smile.

"Guess what?" Phoebe said when Tommy paused. "Our baby is a boy."

"Really?"

Phoebe nodded and couldn't contain her smile.

"Did you hear that?" Tommy exclaimed to everyone in attendance with a huge grin. "I'm having a boy!"

The family members clapped and whistled, as did the priest, and even Johnny managed a smile, but Tommy's mother still looked skeptical. He imagined she wouldn't fully lose her doubt until the baby was in her arms.

———◆———

Violet knew she had almost lost Tommy, so she hurried to him. What Tommy had done for his now-wife, the arson at Marie Russo's shop, didn't surprise her. She knew her son would do anything for the women he held close to him. But that he had keep it a secret from his own mother irked her.

She glanced at Camille and Johnny who continued to restrain Isabella. No one knew how to handle her at the moment. They had some ideas, but with the priest present, they couldn't go through with any of them yet.

"Tommy, why didn't you tell me what you did for Phoebe?" she said, taking him aside.

"I didn't want to trouble you. I didn't want you to get involved. You'd just got out of the hospital.

I knew I could handle it."

"Handle it," Violet replied in disbelief. "This crazy woman showed up and almost killed you. You should've thought it through better. If you're gonna commit a crime like that to someone like that, you have to think through all the angles. You have to consider what might go wrong and how to plan for that."

Tommy didn't say anything in reply, but Violet sensed he understood.

"Tommy," Johnny shouted from where he and Camille now stood with Isabella confined between them. "You did that for my daughter and you didn't tell me? We're supposed to be working together."

Camille frowned and said, "That's a big secret to keep, Tommy."

Violet could feel Tommy tensing at her side and she waited to see how Johnny would finish reacting and readied herself to come to her son's defense.

"You must love my daughter a whole fucking lot," Johnny said to Tommy with a grin.

Violet hid her sigh of relief. She didn't fear the couple, but Tommy had come so far that she didn't want anything to knock him down. Anything.

She approached Camille and suggested they talk. Camille left Johnny holding Isabella, while she and Violet went away from the earshot of the priest.

"What do we do with her?" Camille seemed to be thinking aloud about Isabella.

"I know how we can handle her," Violet replied, although it seemed strange for her to be conspiring with the woman who had been her enemy for so many years. "If she's anything like us, then Isabella isn't going away. She'll plague my Tommy and your daughter until her daughter is released and maybe even after. We have to get rid of her."

"If we kill this woman, we can't do it in front of the priest. Because then we'd have to kill the priest, and I'm not killing a fucking priest," Camille said.

"We wait until he leaves," Violet replied. "We lock her in there," she gestured to a shed near the garden. "And then we carry on and have our party and enjoy ourselves because we deserve that. Then when he goes, we get rid of her. This property is so fucking big no one's gonna hear anything. The only thing is Aldo. You think he'll look the other way?"

Camille seemed slightly insulted by the idea that he wouldn't. "He will. He's my mother's husband, for fuck's sake. Aldo knows a lot of dark secrets, and this will just be another one."

"What about the consequences? She's connected to Vito Russo, right?" Violet asked.

"Vito doesn't care about her anymore," Camille spoke with confidence. "And it sounds like their daughter will be in prison for a long time. We can worry about her later."

"I can kill the mother if you want," Violet offered.

"No, we'll both do it. After what she's done, I might enjoy it," Camille said with a soft chuckle.

Violet smiled slightly, knowingly.

They went to Johnny and Camille told him to distract the priest for a moment. Then they took Isabella from his grasp, leading the resisting woman to the shed, as Johnny kept the priest engaged in conversation.

Isabella writhed and hissed. Violet told her to shut her fucking mouth. Inside the shed they found some strong tape.

"What are you gonna do to me?" Isabella demanded to know, but they didn't answer her.

They covered Isabella's mouth with the tape and bound her wrists and ankles.

"Keep quiet or else we'll kill you," Camille lied, because they'd kill her no matter what.

They left the shed and secured the door well.

Then they went on in merriment as before. No one who knew seemed to mind the woman about to be murdered in the shed when it all had concluded. The families enjoyed a fine, delicious meal, then after the cake, a towering white-and-pink delight, was served, everyone gathered around to watch Tommy and Phoebe dance closely together to a classic 60s love song, which Violet hadn't known Tommy liked.

At the end of it all, Johnny waited until the priest's car left the house to hand Camille Isabella's gun. The priest knew them well enough to not ask questions and get involved. He knew to go.

They planned to dump Isabella's car far away.

Camille walked with Violet to the shed, arguing over who would be the one to fire the fatal shot. Some things never changed.

"I'll do it, she came after my daughter," Camille insisted.

"She nearly killed my son," Violet replied.

"We'll each get a turn," Camille concluded.

Violet paused then nodded. For once, they'd agreed on something.

"When it's done, I'll take the gun back to the city with me and drop it in the river," Violet said.

Camille seemed satisfied with the idea. Then she said, "Did you know that Tommy and Phoebe put a down payment on a new house near Johnny and me?"

"I didn't know that, no," Violet said, internally wondering if the other woman was trying to hurt her.

"I'm sure Tommy planned to tell you," Camille said. "You know, Phoebe showed me her pregnancy results from the doctor. I saw how you looked back there, you looked a little surprised. So I wanted to tell you she isn't lying."

Violet still had her doubts about how the situation had played out, but she didn't say anything.

"Phoebe's my daughter, so I know why I want to get rid of this woman," Camille said. "But why are you helping me?"

"She almost killed my son," Violet emphasized. "Besides, getting rid of her means Tommy and Phoebe can be happy. I can see how much he cares for your daughter."

Camille stopped walking and stared at Violet as though she doubted her intentions. "I'm not sure if I can trust you," she said.

"We're related now so you'll just have to," Violet replied, and they continued walking.

THANKS FOR READING. If you enjoyed *Tommy's Turn*, please share your thoughts on Amazon or Goodreads by leaving a review.

ABOUT THE AUTHORS

E.R. Fallon and KJ Fallon know well the gritty city streets of which they write and have understanding of the localized crime world.

Printed in Great Britain
by Amazon